# THICKER THAN WATER

Other books by Penelope Farmer:

*Charlotte Sometimes*
*Emma in Winter*
*The Summer Birds*

# THICKER
# THAN
# WATER

## PENELOPE FARMER

CANDLEWICK PRESS
CAMBRIDGE, MASSACHUSETTS

First U.S. edition 1993
First published in Great Britain in 1989 by
Walker Books Ltd., London.

*Library of Congress Cataloguing-in-Publication Data*
Farmer, Penelope, 1939 –
Thicker than water/Penelope Farmer. — 1st U.S. ed.
"First published in Great Britain in 1989 by Walker Books, Ltd.,
London"—T.p. verso.
Summary: Both Will and his cousin Becky have some
adjusting to do when he comes to live with her family after
his mother's death, especially when the ghost of a child coal
miner begins his insistent haunting of Will.
ISBN 1-56402-178-5
[1. Ghosts—Fiction.   2. Grief—Fiction.
3. Cousins—Fiction.   4. Orphans—Fiction.   5. England—
Fiction.]   I. Title.
PZ7.F2382Th   1993
[Fic]—dc20                          92–53133

10 9 8 7 6 5 4 3 2 1

Printed in the U.S.A.

Candlewick Press
2067 Massachusetts Avenue
Cambridge, Massachusetts 02140

*Blood being thicker than water
this book is for
Judith Macdonald — any time she likes.*

*Also for Ben Lynch and Megan Lynch — now.
Oliver Shorvon, Nicholas Shorvon, and
Kate Farmer, later
and for Emily Shorvon and Sam Pepper, later still.*

# 1

## BECKY

I know where Will thinks this story begins. Where it began for him, anyway: that first night in our house when he woke up in the moonlight and heard the little boy crying. It is, I agree, a scary enough beginning for any story.

The trouble was I never heard the ghost, not then or later. What with one thing and another, the beginning of the story for me was much more ordinary: the evening in March that I first heard about Megan. Via an S.O.S. message, of all things, on the radio, Radio Four, to be exact, just before the six o'clock news.

I always did like S.O.S. messages. Though I didn't usually listen to Radio Four, I'd turn over from Radio Derby sometimes toward six o'clock when I remembered to, especially in the summer; there were more messages then, because of people being on holiday and so on. "Would John Smith, last heard of in Swindon fifteen years ago, get in touch with XXX Hospital, telephone 123, where his mother (or his father, or his brother, or sister, aunt, or uncle) is dangerously ill." Lots of nights, most nights in fact,

there weren't any messages. But when there were —
my mother wouldn't let me watch TV, of course, while
I was doing my homework, but if I was shut up in my
room she couldn't hear the radio — when there were,
it made a change, thinking about the S.O.S. message,
from thinking about my math and English. Did John
Smith ever hear his S.O.S., for instance? If so, did he
ever get in touch? How could you be out of touch with
your family for fifteen whole years, longer than I'd been
on earth? Blood is thicker than water, after all, or so my
mother is always saying.

There were two messages that night in March. The
first one was for some man "touring Cornwall in
a white Ford Escort." He'd only been away three
days; he wasn't interesting at all, apart from his
being crazy enough to tour anywhere in England at
that time of year — still winter, good as. I didn't
even catch his name. But the second name I picked
up all right. It was the same as my mother's before
she married my father. What's more, whoever it was
came from the place where my mother lived before she
married. "Will Margaret Langworth, last heard of in
Leek, Staffordshire, seventeen years ago, get in touch
with the London Hospital, telephone number ..." — I
didn't quite take that one in, apart from the 01
bit — "... where her twin sister, Megan Langworth,
is dangerously ill."

Since my mother, of course, didn't have a twin sister,

it couldn't possibly be for her. All the same, I was intrigued enough to jot the name *Megan Langworth* in my notebook. I often do jot things down, particularly when I'm bored with doing homework — that night it was reading two chapters of crummy *Lord of the Flies,* which I'd read ages ago at my other school. I probably wouldn't be reading it again if I'd gone to boarding school, I thought, instead of the public school in Matlock.

My mother was out that night at one of her classes. By the time she came back it was nearly nine o'clock. I was watching "Dallas," and had forgotten all about Megan Langworth, whoever she was. In fact, I didn't think another thing about her till two or three days later, when I was looking up something in my notebook and saw the name scrawled there. I couldn't imagine who it was at first. That evening, though, just out of interest, I did mention her to my mother.

We were in the kitchen at the time. In what had been our nice, ordinary kitchen, until Dad, a bit before his business troubles started, insisted they got in an interior designer and did it up along with the rest of the house. It used to have blue Formica shelves and linoleum on the floor. Now, between its low ceiling and quarry tiles, its varnished wooden shelves and stainless steel surfaces, its arrays of shiny knives and shinier saucepans on racks, its dishwasher and its food processor, it looked like a cross between a farmhouse and a factory. I don't know

if Mum liked it any more than I did. She didn't choose
it herself; she's not interested in things like that. In
fact, I'm not sure she wouldn't just as soon have kept
the whole house the way it had been since we moved
in, when I was little. I do know that it cost a ton. I
also know we almost had to move out, and with all
the troubles we might still have to.

The interior designer had let us keep the stove,
fortunately. Or rather, she'd only exchanged it for
one fueled by gas instead of coal, meaning that no
one had to clomp in and out of the door night and
morning carrying hods of coal and trays of ashes, letting
in cold air and dogs, and a lot of bad temper. Apart
from missing the slightly bitter smell of the burning
coal, that was one change I didn't mind much; in front
of the stove was still the coziest place in the house.
I spent half my life hugging it, and so did our two
Labrador dogs, Soldier and Sailor. I was hugging it
now, watching my mother at the steel-topped wooden
table chopping up steak and kidney for a pie.

There was blood, of course, all over her fingers. But
the way she reacted to the name *Megan Langworth,* the
blood mightn't have belonged to some poor slaughtered
animal, it might have been her own. (Or mine.) She
reached out and grabbed my shoulders, blood and all.
I was still wearing my blue-and-white-checked school
blouse, which I am supposed to change the moment
I come in from school, but she had been too busy

chopping to notice. She should have noticed now; she was staring at me directly, holding my eyes like an interrogator in a spy film. But she didn't.

"WHAT did you say?" She was shouting. My big, bossy, busy mother who never shouted, though she had gotten a mite less big, perhaps, since people stopped wanting to buy the bras and vests Dad's Nottingham firm made. "WHAT did you say?"

"I said . . . and *your* name was Margaret Langworth." I stammered between terror and anger. Just when had my mother ever behaved like this?

"Not that. The other one . . ."

"Megan Langworth."

"And the hospital. Don't you remember the name of the hospital?"

"Some London place. How should I know. I don't know. Who's Megan Langworth? You haven't got a twin sister."

"Oh, no?" said my mother, still staring straight into my eyes as if she wanted to turn me into stone. She almost had turned me into stone by now. Except that I was beginning to cry from sheer surprise and fright, and most stones don't weep. "Oh, no. The hospital — you must remember what the hospital was called."

But I couldn't remember. So she went away to ring the B.B.C. and presumably they told her the name and number because I heard her dialing and then speaking again. And after a while she came back, as white as

11

the moment before she had been red, and said, "You're quite right, I haven't got a sister. She's dead. If not buried. If I've not missed the funeral ..." She hesitated then. I could almost see the words forming on her lips. "It's no thanks to you." But she didn't say them. Just as well, I thought. How could she be so unfair? Instead, she made me fetch the bottle of brandy from the cupboard next door and pour her out a glass. Then she went on cutting up steak and kidney furiously, as if she didn't know what she was doing. Or as if she was cutting me up. Once she said, almost pleadingly, "Why didn't you tell me?"

"It didn't seem to matter," I said. "I didn't know. How could I? You never told me." And she said, "Of course not," in a brisk voice, took the slab of pastry, rolled it out as heavily and indifferently as a steamroller rolling a road, put it on the meat, pinched the edges, and set the dish in the oven, brushing me out of the way to do so. Then she looked at me again. This time she said, "Why haven't you changed out of your uniform? And what have you gone and gotten on your shoulders?"

"Steak and kidney," I answered, craning my neck to find the blood. "Blood," I added, as if she didn't know. Whereupon she repeated, so mechanically it mightn't have been her speaking at all but rather an old machine that insisted on repeating such things, "What are you doing still wearing your school uniform?"

She opened the oven door again and slammed it shut; perhaps she was afraid of not having shut it properly the first time. Then she went away and did a lot more telephoning — I don't know who to. She closed the door to the study so that I couldn't hear. And then my father came in and she spent a long time talking to him. By the time we ate the steak and kidney pie it was burned at the edges. Moreover we ate it by itself, without vegetables, nothing, not even potatoes. Such a thing never happened — everything was always done properly in our house. They'd even gone on being done properly when Dad's bras and panties were doing so badly it looked as if he would go bankrupt any minute. But not tonight. Apart from there being no vegetables, my mother had just thrown the knives and forks and things on the table. She hadn't put out the napkins in their silver rings.

It didn't matter. Neither of them seemed very hungry, even my dad who likes his food so much that he's fat, not just big like Mum, though not nearly as fat as he used to be before his business troubles started. I ate most of that steak and kidney. Being miserable always made me want to eat; that's why I've put on so much weight since I started going to public school. (My mother says it's just Puberty, with a capital $P$ — she doesn't know about the sweets and buns I gobble during break and after school.) Not that it helped. I went up to bed feeling as puzzled and miserable as ever, the more so when I heard Dad start shouting behind me — something about "that tart" and "What's dead's better left buried." He seemed angrier about the whole thing than anything, not really sad and upset, like Mum.

But he went down to London next day with my mother, just the same. The nice thing about my parents is that they always do back each other up in matters concerning their families. Blood is thicker than water, my mother says, often, though I have to add that it didn't stop them from leaving this bit of their flesh and blood in the lurch, and not for the first time, either. By which I mean I had to go and stay the night with our nearest neighbors. Their daughter is nearly the same age as me, and they think we ought to be friends. But we're not.

A few days later, my mother went down to London again, again with my father, but wearing a black coat. She went to the funeral, I suppose, but she didn't say. And I didn't ask. For one thing I almost didn't want to know; for another I wasn't used to asking questions. I'd never had to much before, as my mother always believed in telling me things before I got round to asking. "Keeping you in the picture," she called it. "Not beating about the bush."

She'd never hidden the facts of life from me, for instance, any more than she hid Dad's money problems when they started. What's more, she always spoke when she was explaining such things to me very loudly and slowly and clearly, pretty much as if she were addressing the Women's Institute or a committee meeting, or one of the classes she went to in the evenings to learn about local history and so forth. She was never the least bit embarrassed, the way other people said their parents were. But I was.

This time, though, when she did finally get round to telling me what was happening, the day after the funeral, I was much less embarrassed than my mother. I was angry, mainly. "Why didn't you tell me any of this before?" I first begged then shouted at her, over and over. But she never answered. She went on saying what she wanted to say so haltingly, in such a low voice, not looking at me directly, that I had the impression she would still have preferred to keep me in the dark about Megan. But of course she couldn't anymore, what with the S.O.S. message, what with this new boy cousin she suddenly produced from nowhere, between one sentence and the next. He was in a foster home at the moment, apparently. He'd been in a foster home already before his mother died; she hadn't been in a position to look after him herself, my mother explained. She'd had one or two problems.

It was a miserable evening, and we were both hugging the stove this time. The clocks had already been put forward for summer time. At seven o'clock it was still light outside, so we weren't spared the sight of the rain and cold and the bare trees beyond the window.

"His name's Will," my mother said. "I hope he'll be coming up to stay with us, once the papers have been sorted out. His mother said it's what she wanted, before she died."

"How long's he going to stay, then?" I asked, half pleased and half appalled. After all, I'd never had a cousin before, except for one in Australia whose parents had forgotten how old I was and still sent me things like toy kangaroos for Christmas, every other year or so.

I was even more appalled and not at all pleased when she replied, "Well, duck, we — I — was hoping he might stay permanently with us. If he wants to. Of course, it's up to him."

She hesitated, she stumbled, she still didn't look at me. She looked out the window. She looked at the brass clock on the wall opposite the stove. Was this how other people's mothers told their children the facts of life? I wondered, glancing at her surreptitiously. Worse still, she added, "I hope in due course, Becky, he might even be a brother to you. At least" (I suppose she saw my face), "at least *like* a brother to you."

"How could he be my brother?" I retorted coldly. "We haven't got the same mother. He can't ever be anything except my cousin. Even if blood is thicker than water."

16

It wasn't him I blamed for any of this, of course, not really. I felt sorry for him if anything. It was her I was angry with, her I blamed for not telling me about Megan. Because all her talk about "keeping me in the picture" and "not beating about the bush" was a complete lie. She'd beaten about every bush. She hadn't given me any of the real picture, or at least only the half of the picture that had her in it. In the other half my mother had a twin sister who had run away at seventeen and never come back. In fact, she hadn't been heard of at all since she was twenty.

I, too, meanwhile, as she told me all this, was mostly staring at the big brass clock on the far wall. Every now and then, though, I stole a glance at her. She didn't look so very different from the way she'd always looked, I thought, even if she was behaving differently. She was wearing the same old blue fisherman's sweater she usually wore at home in the winter. On her feet were a pair of slipper socks. How big her feet are, I thought. Perhaps, till now, I'd always taken her too much for granted to realize quite how big they were. Perhaps as time went on I was going to notice other things about her that I'd never noticed, that I'd much rather not notice.

From now on, for instance, was I going to keep imagining that she was still hiding something from me? I wondered. She wasn't telling me the whole truth now, for a start. When she told me Megan got into trouble in London, she didn't get round to saying what kind of trouble it could have been or what kind of problems Megan had had since to prevent her from looking after Will. Suddenly I stopped looking at her feet or out the window or at the big brass clock. I stared her straight in the face and asked coldly, "You mean she was a junkie? Or she kept having abortions? Or what?"

Oh, yes, I could imagine the kind of problems Megan might have encountered and gone on encountering in London. I'm not blind. I'm not deaf. Even if my mother hadn't yet filled me in in these areas, I listen to the radio, watch television, see the papers — who doesn't? "John Smith, last heard of twenty years ago ..." Oh, yes, if it had never seemed before to have anything to do with me, I knew all about that, and I was going to put my mother in the picture all right, to show her just what I knew. With her, with my mother, I didn't intend doing any beating about the bush.

Not that it was going to stop anything, of course. It didn't. And it was all much worse than I could possibly have imagined. Will, my cousin, arrived in the end, though it took much longer than my mother had expected. She had to go down to London lots of times to see him — I should have gone once or twice, but I always managed to get out of it. And it was the summer holidays before the day came when he stood at last, in Derby station, just off the train, a little wretched shrimp of a boy a whole head shorter than me. How dare such a little shrimp of creature, I was thinking, be my cousin? How could anyone so foreign looking, with his black eyes and black hair, with his not entirely pink Midlands skin like my mother's and mine, be my cousin? Who was his father, then? I wondered for the first time. No one had ever so much as mentioned his father.

Meanwhile he stood there staring and not staring at me, in the same way as I was staring and not staring at him, at his raincoat — he wore a raincoat even though it was a hot summer day — at his gray school trousers, and at his worldly goods clutched to his middle in a red squashy bag.

(I asked him later if they were all his worldly goods. He claimed that they were. I was so appalled I almost offered to give him my Walkman on the spot. But of course I didn't.)

# 2

## W I L L

It was the social worker, Ms. Simms, who told me I had a cousin, not to mention that I had an aunt and an uncle. This was the same Ms. Simms as told me my mother died. I didn't like being told things by her.

But in fact she was OK, that social worker, as they go, dangly earrings, duffel bag, and all, even if she did try a few times to make me call her Wendy instead of Ms. Simms, even if she was nearly crying when she told me about my mother. Social workers aren't supposed to cry, are they? Well, maybe not, but this one did.

It was Ms. Simms, too, who took me to the station to catch the train to Derby. She bought me football papers, out of her own pocket, as if I was interested in football, which she ought by now to know I'm not. But how's she supposed to remember everything, with all the nutcases like me she's supposed to deal with? And I don't think her mind was on the job, any more than mine was. (Anyway, I didn't need nothing. Mr. Milsom, my foster father, had given me a science fiction paperback as a good-bye present, an Isaac Asimov I'd read before, but it didn't matter.) She told me to be sure not to get off at Wellingborough or Leicester or Long Eaton.

"It's Derby where you have to get off, Will," she said. "Don't forget."

"What happens if I don't get off?" I asked her, looking at the picture of Gary Lineker scoring a goal for Barcelona. "Suppose I go on to Sheffield, for instance?" (The train went as far as Sheffield. It said so on the big electronic board above our heads.) "Or suppose I get off at Leicester?"

"You'll just give everyone a lot of trouble. Not least yourself. Who do you know in Leicester or Sheffield?"

"Who do I know in Derby?" I said. "Aside from the fact that she's called Aunt?"

"Oh, come off it, Will. No one's making you go there. You chose to. And you know it's only a trial, to see how you like it."

Which was true, in a way. So I didn't stay on the train till Sheffield. Though when we'd been stopped at Leicester a minute or two, and the bloke in a turban opposite me suddenly jumped up in a hurry as if he'd been thinking about something else and not noticed where we were, I watched him get out, watched him walk away down the platform and imagined myself lugging my red squashy bag after him, out the door, down the steps, between the trolleys and packages stacked up on the platform, past the bookstall, out of the red brick station, into the red brick town.

But then it was too late; the door slammed, a whistle blew, and the train started to move. And the skies got bigger, it seemed to me, and the fields greener, and there was great curved cooling towers and belches of smoke, like the ones I could see from the North London Line at Willesden the times Mum took me to Kew Gardens, which she was allowed to sometimes, and to other places, museums and things, even if she wasn't allowed to have me to live with her all the time.

Seeing those cooling towers was the nearest I got to crying that day or most others. But these towers didn't stay so far off. Soon they sat up against us, they looked like beer mugs for giants the way they was foaming at the top; I forgot about crying then. Or maybe I didn't. Maybe I just decided against it. I picked up the football papers instead and tore them into little shreds and threw them out the window. So much for Gary Lineker and Nigel Clough, the whole bloody lot of them. So much for Long Eaton, which was the place we came to next, not that I could have gotten out there — the train didn't even stop, and anyway it wasn't no proper station at all, only a little platform.

So what do you know, Ms. Simms? I thought, eyeing the Isaac Asimov, which was all about a man who could move around in eternity and change the present or the future, just by shifting a box a millimeter or two in an earlier time, for instance, or just by crushing a butterfly's wing. (That's what I like about science fiction — everything's possible there, not like life, where most things aren't.) So much for you, Ms. Simms.

Next thing the West Indian voice on the Tannoy was saying, "Derby. This train is approaching Derby." And there, standing on the platform of yet another red brick station, was my aunt, who I recognized, just about, from the times she'd been to see me since Mum died; and my cousin Becky, who I didn't, a stubby-looking girl with frizzy brown hair and snippy-snappy brown eyes, wearing a miniskirt for which she was a bit too fat, I'm glad to say, likewise for the T-shirt, which said Dire Straits, quite rightly, across her front. But then she didn't seem no more pleased to see me than I was pleased to see her. It'd be hard to say, assuming there was a competition, which of us gave the smallest, most suspicious smiles, like Big Daddy was about to lay into the Mighty Midget. (Wrestling, I mean.) When Aunt Maggie kissed me, Becky retreated a good step or two and stopped smiling altogether. She might have been afraid she would have to kiss me too. As if I would have let her.

She wasn't even pretty, for a start, besides being bigger than me and fat. She wasn't as big as my aunt, though — what a sight we must have been when she bent down and kissed me, like an elephant lumbering on a gnat. I sneaked a look at Becky in the meantime, gave a little wriggle, made a little face, to see if I could get a rise out of her. But if she did find us a bit of a laugh, she wasn't going to show it, was she, not her. Soon as she noticed me looking she flicked back her hair, hitched up her skirt, and stared in the other direction.

Being from London, I'm used to towns going on forever. To my amazement we was out of Derby before you could say knife, though we did pass the back of several other little towns. One had a red brick factory with a huge chimney looking down at green fields. I didn't know much about the country. I expected it to be different from a town, that's all. I mean, I didn't expect to see green fields mixed up with factory chimneys.

I'd noticed before, in London, how much Aunt Maggie liked explaining things, more like a teacher than an aunt, let alone a mum, *my* mum anyway. Now she told me who the factory had been founded by, Josiah Someone, taking her left hand off of the wheel, as usual, to point at it, and looking every which way, except at the road. God help all the other drivers, I thought. God help me.

I didn't take none of it in. Not with Becky so close behind me, leaning her elbows on the back of my seat, breathing down my neck, not saying a word. She couldn't have heard no word, neither. She had a Walkman on — I could hear a little tinny thread of sound coming out of it, I could feel her jigging ever so slightly to a beat I couldn't hear. Aunt Maggie suddenly stopped looking at the road and turned to yell at her.

"Take that Walkman off, Becky. I thought I told you to leave it at home. If you're not careful I'll confiscate the thing for the rest of the holidays."

"It's only so I don't have to listen to the lectures," Becky muttered, loud enough for me to hear but not her mother, which made me wonder if it was me coming she was so fed up with, after all. Maybe it was more her mother.

We turned off the main road then and went up through the green fields, like we was leaving the world behind. The walls of the fields was made of stone and so was the walls of the house we got to. The house was like a wall. I mean, it took up where the wall left off, it made the wall along the road itself, fronting right onto it, there wasn't no yard, no foot of garden, nothing. One of its windows was so close to the ground you'd barely have had to lift a foot six inches to put it through the glass. The front door didn't open onto the road, though. To reach that you had to go in at an iron gate and turn sharp left, past a big stone pot with some sort of red flowers growing in it, past two big yellowish dogs who got to their feet and followed us, waggling their tails, sniffing at our backsides, rude like.

It wasn't like no other place I'd ever lived in. Those places was always brick houses or concrete flats. Plus

I'd always lived in towns, whereas there didn't seem to be so much as a village here that I could see, just a wall and a house and a garden, another house or two up the hill opposite, a bad smell — "That's the pig farm," Becky said, but I couldn't see it — and a little wood over the road, at the top of which a load of great black birds was yelling and fussing.

"Listen to the rooks," Becky said as we got out of the car. "What's gotten into them?" And it was true that they was making racket enough, but it weren't the sort of racket I was used to. I was used to cars and trains and planes and things, day and night. The rooks was like a silence to me. I mean they was like a silence, comparatively speaking.

No more I wasn't used to the kind of house I found myself stepping into, through a door I'd have banged my head on, was I six foot tall. A house full of polished wooden chairs and chests and tables and matching chairs and sofas with fringed covers, and pale pictures in thin gold frames. (My mother never had no furniture to speak of — we ate off our knees instead of a table. She always slept on a mattress on the floor.)

There was a fringed cover on the bed in the room to which me and my red bag followed Becky, one of the big yellow dogs (they was called Soldier and Sailor; I couldn't tell them apart) still hard at our heels. Up a narrow, creaky little staircase we went, turning right past a huge wooden wardrobe, along a narrow, creaky little passage. The door had a wooden latch instead of a knob, which clacked when Becky pulled it up and let it down again. The two gold-framed pictures hanging on the walls was of flowers, roses, and suchlike. The little window opposite the door looked out on the wood and the squalling black birds. It didn't look like a room full of ghosts. Not that I imagined those kinds of ghosts at that moment — why should I?

I stood and stared out the window for a bit. So did Becky. Without her mother she didn't seem to know what to say to me, no more did I know what to say to her. Nor she didn't seem to know whether she wanted to stay in the room or go away, nor I didn't know whether I wanted her to go or stay, neither. But when I turned round I found her staring at me. Then I did want her to go, even though she tried at once to pretend she hadn't been staring. She tugged down her skirt, not that it made the slightest bit of difference, you could still see she had great fat hams, pushed her hair back, and said, "Do you want some tea? Mum's making some." And before I had time to say what I was going to, which was, "You'll know me on a dark night now, won't you?" she grabbed the yellow dog by the collar and almost ran out of the room, blushing, letting the wooden latch clack behind her. Even if she hadn't run, I don't suppose I'd've said anything when it came to it. I didn't feel like saying nothing to no one very much.

Hearing her footsteps creak away along the passage, I sat down on the bed, on the fringed cover with its daisies and buttercups, which matched not only the cover on the little armchair but the cover of the box of tissues on the dressing table in front of the mirror, and wondered how my thin mother and my fat aunt could be so different, apart from their both being tall. They was twins, wasn't they? I was thinking. Oughtn't they to be the same? There'd been girl twins at one of the schools I went to, they was so alike, no one had ever known which of them was which.

For one wild and hopeful moment when Ms. Simms first told me about Aunt Maggie, I'd imagined she'd be as exactly like my mum as those twins was like one another, only a bit less hopeless, at least able to look after herself. If I'm honest it's what I really held against Mum; not that she couldn't look after me, not even her taking up with that bloody Mike and what he did to me; not even the fact that she hadn't, never, told me about my dad; but that she couldn't, proper, look after herself — that was what got her onto the stuff she called her "happy pills," and so forth.

But it wasn't like that, was it? It never is. Aunt Maggie was as big and fat as my mother was so thin you could see through her, good as. Aunt Maggie talked as much as my mother didn't, mostly. Never mind that she was downstairs at this very minute making my tea as any good mum should. I sat in this low stone house, with its walls thick enough to keep out the world and the weather and men from outer space, listening to those rooks cawing and a silence I wasn't used to, feeling such miles from nowhere, I might as well have been in outer space, or eternity for that matter, like the man in the Isaac Asimov book, who could look at the future and if he saw things going wrong in it change the past.

If only someone could have done that for me, I thought. If only someone in the past could have looked at my future and, not liking what he saw, changed one tiny thing about. Then my mother wouldn't have run away, nor met Mike, nor killed herself in the end. Then she could have been an ordinary mother, always there when I wanted, in fact around for my whole life. She always said she loved me, didn't she? After she died, Ms. Simms told me she really had, that she'd made herself ill with sadness, not because she hadn't loved me enough. I wanted to believe her. Every once in a while I could have believed the pair of them. Every once in a while I couldn't.

Well, that was the way I felt, though it was still daylight then and I was listening to cawing rooks and creaking stairs, expecting a hot cup of tea any moment. I'd not even heard yet the dreadful crying in the night.

I was very tired that evening. I went to sleep almost as soon as I got into bed, though I didn't expect to. Outside, through the deep little window, it still wasn't quite dark, and the rooks over the road was still muttering a bit.

I don't think I was asleep for very long, though. Just long enough for the rooks to fall silent, for it to get quite dark, and for the moon to come up and start shining in at my window. Then something woke me quite suddenly, dragging me out of a deep dream about my mum. I didn't know what it was at first. But after a minute my senses came back, I recognized the sound of someone — a little kid, I thought, a boy — I don't know why I was so sure it was a boy, but I was, even then — crying his heart out.

It wasn't the first time in my life I'd been kept awake by someone crying. In two of my foster homes there'd been babies cried all night. But this one — I felt quite kindly to it at first, since it woke me from a dream I'd much rather not have been having — this one wasn't like that. It wasn't a baby, for a start. And it didn't cry all the time; it stopped and started; stopped and started. Sometimes it made screams and howls like it was being murdered. And sometimes — and that was worse — it made a kind of low grumbling, just went on and on, like the hope was gone in the world and that was that.

All this didn't make me feel sorry for whoever it was who was crying. After a bit it just made me feel sorrier for myself. I stopped feeling kindly toward it;

all I wanted was to give the person concerned a good kicking.

Who was it anyway, this kid? No one didn't say nothing about a kid. Did I have another cousin as well as Becky? If so, I liked the sound of it even less than I liked her. Why hadn't I stayed with Mr. and Mrs. Milsom, I wondered, lying rigid under the green-and-white-flowered duvet, which felt much too hot suddenly, but which I didn't like to kick off; it seemed protection of some sort, assuming I needed protection from whatever it was letting rip with those heart-rending sobs. I could have stayed with the Milsoms. Mr. Milsom got some science fiction books out of the library for me when he heard I liked them. He'd gotten me a library card even. No one hadn't never done that for me before. In fact, I'd liked Mr. Milsom so much that sometimes, not knowing about my real dad, I'd even wished he was my real dad, instead of whoever he was.

I mean, it's not like I'll ever know who my real dad was. My mother had said she might tell me about him when I was older, but she can't now, can she? Maybe I'd rather not know — she was quite enough for one person to be going on with. Though I'd been called a Paki at school a few times, I don't think he was a Paki, more like Greek or Turkish or something. I know my mother went to Turkey once. She had a funny hat she said she bought in Istanbul.

I opened my eyes after a bit. I couldn't see much

at first, it being dark, and though there was a light by my bed, which was another thing I'd never had in all my life, I didn't fancy turning it on somehow. Once my eyes got used to things, I didn't need to anyway. The moonlight was very bright. At least I'd seen the moon before, I thought, if it did slink its mean way here through walls so thick you could hide in the windowsill. Which looked like what the moon was doing. It was as sneaky as Ms. Simms was when she'd told me my mum had just died, or rather topped herself; taken a few too many of her happy pills, that is. Definitely sneaky, she'd been — not quite looking at me, like she was afraid I'd cry, maybe, or maybe was afraid I wouldn't. Which I didn't, not when she was around, leastways, though not to make things easier for her. (But not to make things easier for me, neither.)

Nor was I going to cry now. No, I wasn't. "Shut up, shut up," I hissed, at last, sitting up in bed. Whereupon to my surprise and even terror, the kid did shut up, or seemed to. Maybe it was just worn out and drawing a deep breath. There was silence, anyway. But such a heavy silence it was almost worse, I could hardly bear it. Looking at the moonlight slinking in, I jumped out of bed and ran toward it. I climbed into the windowsill and sat looking out at the trees in the wood across the road.

And then the crying started again. And there was I with nothing between it and me but the air and the moonlight, plus a space of empty floor between me and my bed and my duvet that I didn't dare cross, though I longed to.

Not even my own things looked familiar now. My red bag, sitting on the armchair with the flowery cover, wasn't red but silver gray, and so was the buttercups and daisies on the chair cover. The bed, reflected in the mirror, didn't look like no bed no longer. And the door — I looked at the door in the mirror too, I was so stiff with fright I couldn't manage to turn my head to look properly, the door, wasn't it moving? Couldn't I hear, behind the wails, a small wooden scraping on the carpet? Hadn't I shut it properly before I went to bed? Why hadn't I? I wondered.

"Stop your noise," I begged the yelling kid. "Please. Oh, please. Bloody stop your noise. You're going to set me off if you're not careful. Bloody stop, will you? Just let me listen." Because it was, certainly, not just crying I could hear now. In response to my pleas or not, the crying was beginning to die away; a panting, a snuffling, a heavy breathing sound was taking its place. The door began, quite definitely, shifting. This was altogether too much for me. I launched myself, rather than jumped, off the windowsill, scuttled into the bed, and buried my head under the duvet.

Next thing I knew, a great heavy shape had gone and landed on me. I thought I was going to die for a moment. I was whimpering with terror until suddenly I felt the friendliness of the thing, allowed myself to recognize what it was. Dared poke my head out, cautiously, from under.

Now I've never had much to do with dogs in my life, but I've always quite liked them. The moment I knew it was only a yellow dog, Soldier or Sailor, flopping all over me, smiling at me almost in the moonlight, rubbing its wet nose into my hand that was still sweaty and trembling with terror, I knew it was all right. I was even grateful for a faceful of its smelly breath. The crying had stopped, anyway. I couldn't hear so much as a whimper. I dared get out of bed after a bit and shut the door to stop the dog from leaving me abandoned. Not that it seemed to want to abandon me. In the morning its weight still lay across my feet.

I don't know whether the crying started up again at some point. But if it did, I never heard it. I only know that I woke to find a dazzle of daylight reflected off the trees, to find Soldier or Sailor smiling at me again, thumping his tail on the bedcover, his moist pink tongue hanging out over his black gums, making even his teeth look friendly. I could almost have believed I'd dreamed the whole thing, that there hadn't never been a little kid crying like the world was lost to the both of us. But I didn't dare believe it, quite.

# 3

## BECKY

My cousin didn't look any better at breakfast next morning than he had when he arrived. If anything, wearing jeans and a T-shirt instead of school clothes, he looked worse. His jeans were so loose on him that he appeared smaller and thinner than ever. Also he said the strangest thing. Was he crazy on top of everything else? I wondered. My mother didn't hear it; she had gone out of the dining room for a moment to catch the postman, when suddenly he turned to me and whispered — I can't do his London accent any more than he could probably do mine, as I've let myself get more and more Derbyshire since I started going to public school, mostly because I can see it annoys my mother — "'Aven't you got a little brother or somefing? Where do you keep 'im? Ain't I going to meet 'im too?"

I stared at him, blankly. "Whatever do you mean?" I said. "Of course I haven't got a little brother." He made faces then and pretended it was all a joke. Turning things into a joke seemed to be usual with him — he did the same at the station yesterday, for instance, when my mother bent to kiss him. But I was determined not to let him see that he could make me laugh.

It was really very awkward, having him around. Even without him asking silly questions about little brothers, etc., I didn't know what to do about it, except behave badly. I did behave badly over the next few days, I admit. If I look at it sensibly it was probably clever of my mother to take us round sightseeing and so forth. Anything had to be better than Will and me sitting at home looking at each other, with me remembering all that stuff I'd been told about visitors, how you ought to look after them, and be nice, and so on. Will might have been my cousin but he still seemed like a visitor; he went on seeming like a visitor for quite a long time after.

Not that I was nice to him, exactly, as my mother took us here, there, and everywhere; from the Tram Museum up at Crich, to the museum at Derby, to the caves up at Castleton, to the cable car at Matlock Bath. Actually we didn't get on the cable car in the end, as the queue was too long when we got there, and I made a great fuss about waiting.

But then I made a fuss about everything it was possible to make any kind of fuss about. I couldn't stop myself. There might have been some horrible little demon inside me, inhabiting my voice. If I sat in the back of the car I felt sick — I said. If I sat in the front it gave me a headache — I said. If Will opened his window I complained it was too windy. If he shut it I complained it was too hot. I grumbled that I didn't like tunnels. ("They make me feel claustrophobic" — well, they do, a bit.) That I didn't like caves. ("It's like being inside a huge stomach." Well, it is, a bit.) I said mines were creepy (which they are, if you think of the poor miners working down there day after day and often dying young). All the way round that huge house, Chatsworth, I muttered, not quite beneath my breath, "Boring, boring, boring." (It is, as a matter of fact.) I stated, several times over, that the Tram Museum wasn't nearly as good as the Transport Museum in London. (It isn't.)

It didn't help that my mother kept up her teacher act most of the time, telling us about the geology and so on. I'm afraid I was nastier about that than about almost anything — at least I was when I heard her — and a lot of the time I kept my Walkman playing so that I couldn't.

"I suppose that information came from your course on the landscape of Derbyshire," I'd say, as nastily as I knew how to. Or, "Was that your class on the history of lead mining?" Or whatever.

I don't know why she didn't bash me for being so obnoxious. I would have. She never used to let me get away with things like that. I wished she wouldn't let me get away with it now, if I'm honest. Not that Will would have noticed how all this business seemed to have changed her. Perhaps that's why I kept going on at her, hoping she'd go back to being how she was, and feeling lonelier and lonelier every time she didn't.

It was on the third day that we went up to Castleton, where all the biggest caves are.

I'd been in some of the caves before, of course, but not for ages. I'd forgotten what they were really like, which really is like someone's insides, I'm sorry to say. All pink and white and yellow, all pointed and rounded. Like tripes and guts and lungs and livers. With slimy yellowy white bits just like the outside of a suet pudding. Yuck. To make it worse, you had to go round the caves in parties with other people, led by guides who made endless stupid jokes about people banging their heads on fossils, and rocks throwing shadows that looked like the face of a nasty schoolteacher. Or about people falling over seven stalagmites (that's the ones on the ground, it's stalactites that hang down from the ceiling) named after the Seven Dwarfs.

I was much more interested myself in thinking about the people who found the caves in the first place. Of course, they wouldn't have walked on the concrete paths. Of course, all the stalactites and things wouldn't have been lit with floodlights for them. They must really have thought they were going down into the center of the earth.

It did still feel a bit like setting out for the center of the earth, in spite of the concrete and floodlights. At the deepest point of the farthest cave they let you into, you could see a tunnel going on down, deeper and deeper. The concrete steps stopped at that point. There was a railing to prevent you going any farther.

Will seemed more fascinated by this than anything. He stood for ages holding on to the railing, peering down into the tunnel.

"Didn't you never read *Journey to the Center of the Earth?*" he asked me. "You know, by Jules Verne."

"I read it in a comic once," I said. "It was dire. All science fiction is dire. All those people called things like Smurg and Viconia and Dunt. And being lost in eternity and outer space. The thought of getting lost between home and Matlock is bad enough."

"Think of being lost in the middle of the earth right under your feet, what no one knows nothing about," he said, sounding excited. "Right under your very feet. Suppose you went on down there. And got beyond all them hot bits and fires and things, and found a great sea like in Jules Verne. With all kinds of extinct creatures roaming around. Ichthyosaurs and plesiosaurs and things."

It was the first time since he'd arrived that he'd said much more than three words together. Certainly the first time he'd even hinted at a way of talking that I got quite used to later, mixing Cockney, bad grammar, and stuff that might have come out of a book. Not that I took much notice of it then.

"I'd rather not think of it," I said. "In any case, he wouldn't find any ichy whatevers. You'd just be another lost potholer on the TV news. Especially if they didn't find you till you were dead."

"Like to bet?" he said. And then, to my horror, he started to climb over the railing, as if he were really going to start journeying to the center of the earth. He was fooling around, of course. He was trying to stir me up and anyone else who saw him. Only there wasn't anyone else to see him. The guide had stopped making jokes about the millions of years it took stalactites to join up with stalagmites — "Anyone for infinity, boys and girls, ladies and gents" — and he was leading the rest of the party, mostly kids with their mothers, like us, back up the concrete steps toward the cave above.

"Don't, Will," I said. But he just winked at me. And now he was actually on the other side of the railing with its big notice saying NO PUBLIC ACCESS BEYOND THIS POINT. "Will, *don't*."

I glanced desperately behind me. And still no one else had seen what was happening. I wanted to call someone back. From the grin on his face I thought he was only fooling, but I couldn't any longer be quite sure. Suppose he did, actually, keep on going? Suppose I had to follow after him, into that deep throat, which looked darker and scarier the more I looked at it? Maybe there could really be ichywhatsits down there, not to mention rivers and steep drops and never-ending darkness. Who would want to leave their bones in a cave like that? Too many people around these parts had, I knew all too well, left their bones in caves and potholes. Miners, potholers, whatever. There was some child, for instance, supposed to have gone down a mine shaft over our way and never come out, a century or two ago. Some even said that on dark nights you could hear him crying. Which was nonsense, of course — I don't believe in ghosts. All the same, it wasn't a nice story.

And then, at that very moment, with Will still the wrong side of the rails, grinning at me like a demon, all the lights went out. And from the cave above some child started crying; worse, almost screaming. It was really creepy, I admit. Great wails and sobs echoed and echoed all round us, as though the cave had grown both bigger and smaller at the same time.

I felt something clutching me, all of a sudden. I heard gasps and sighing close up to my very ear, and let out a great yell myself, just as the lights went on again. In fact they couldn't have been off for more than a minute or two. But there was a ghost, of a sort — my cousin Will. It's true everyone looks a peculiar color down there, what with the yellow floodlight and so on, but it was nothing like the way he looked, he was so white, hanging on to me, his mouth and eyes wide open.

"What's up, Will? It was only a little boy crying. The one in the Snoopy T-shirt? Can't you see him?"

I shook him off. It was all very embarrassing. It was

41

even more embarrassing when the guide in his jeans and
sneakers came loping back down, winked at the sight of
us, and said, "How's your boyfriend then? Making t'
most of t' lights going out?"

"He's not my boyfriend," I said indignantly. "He's
just my little cousin."

He winked again. "That's what they all say, darling.
If you're nice to me, I won't tell your mum."

I wouldn't speak to Will after that. I had a right to be
angry with him now, I thought, for making such a fool
of me. When we were talking earlier I'd even thought
I would lend him my Walkman that afternoon, but I
didn't. Not after that. Anyone would think, seeing his
face, that he had heard a ghost. But how could anyone,
not crazy, have thought the little boy in the Snoopy
T-shirt was a ghost? Maybe he just thought he heard
the ichywhatsits coming up out of the tunnel to get
him.

The next day my mother had a meeting, so she
didn't take us anywhere. I mooched around in my
room all morning instead, still so angry with Will
that I didn't want anything to do with him. I couldn't
not see him, though. He stayed in the garden, in full
sight of my window, under the apple tree near my
old swing, reading one of his disgusting science fiction
books. Sometimes he went on the swing, which is too
low for me now, but not for him. Even so he didn't
use it properly, he made it go all skewwhiff, twisting

and turning it sometimes, round and back, making me feel sick even to look at him. Afterward he lay on the ground and went to sleep, or pretended to. He had his thumb stuck in his mouth then, I noticed to my astonishment, like a baby.

My mother had left some lunch for us in the fridge. I went and got it eventually and took it out to him. A picnic lunch without any grown-ups should have been fun really, but it wasn't. Will hardly ate anything, as usual. If you're inclined to be too fat yourself, eating lunch with someone who won't eat is pretty upsetting. It makes you feel fatter than ever, apart from making you eat more, because you finish up what they don't.

Will's wet, I thought, glowering at his bent head. He's a wimp, a suckathumb baby. He's the wettest, wimpiest boy I ever met in my whole life. Look at him, in the middle of the summer he's not tanned at all, not anywhere. He's so thin you can see his bones. I know I should feel sorry for him, with his dead mother and that. My mother is always telling me I should feel sorry for him. But I don't. Partly because she will keep telling me I should feel sorry for him. Why does my mother always tell me what to feel? I thought, staring at the pathetic ribs and jutting collarbone and sallow skin Will revealed when he took off his T-shirt, muttering something about his being much too hot. Why can't she ever just let me sort out my own feelings for myself?

"Look at you. You don't eat enough to keep a fly alive," I accused him.

"I am a fly," he said. "Ain't you noticed? Nor I'm not dead yet. Maybe you hadn't noticed that, neither."

My mother came back at about four. We were still in the garden then, lying on the ground under the apple tree, both reading or pretending to. (I was reading *Grimms' Fairy Tales* for the umpteenth time — I should have grown out of them by then but I hadn't. Besides, the way I felt, stories about witches coming to nasty ends, such as being rolled downhill in barrels stuck with nails, suited me very well.) At about half past four she brought out a tray of tea things. And also two big books with gilt letters on them that I'd never clapped eyes on before in my life.

"I thought you might like to look at these," she said.

They were photograph albums, both of them, rather dusty. One blue, the other dark red.

"Do you mean," I said, burning with anger suddenly, "do you mean you've had these all the time and never showed me?"

"I'm showing them to you now, duck," she said.

Because of her meeting she wore a neat green-and-white linen suit with a belt and a silver brooch in the shape of a rose pinned on the lapel. She wore white

sandals but no stockings, her toes coming out of the
sandals, at my eye level almost, looked horribly big and
red.

"Are you sure I'm old enough?" I asked coldly. "Are
you sure Will is?"

"What is the matter with you, Rebecca?"

"You should know," I said.

My mother's face now was even redder than her
toes. Is she going to cry? I wondered. I never had
seen my mother cry. The prospect both interested and
appalled me, not least because seeing those big albums,
I imagined a heart I didn't know after all, inside that
familiar green suit. What else didn't I know about her?
I wondered. What else was her head full of that I knew
nothing about?

Will's book about eternity was sitting on the
grass, face downward. I hated the very thought of
eternity — I didn't want to imagine all the hugeness
and emptiness out there. How could he bear to spend
his time reading about such things? But even his head
stuffed with such outlandish matters couldn't seem
stranger than my mother's head seemed to me at that
moment.

Will had opened one of the books already. I resented
my curiosity, but I was curious — how could I not
be? I moved closer to him, to find myself staring at
a dark-haired woman, my grandmother, presumably,
though she hadn't looked like that when I knew her;

her hair was in a tight perm and her lipstick made her mouth appear hard and bright. She was holding a baby on either arm. Which was Megan and which my mother? I couldn't have told; I doubted if my mother could now. I doubted if anyone could.

I'd hardly seen any pictures of my mother before she got married even, let alone any of her as a child. It wasn't till now that it occurred to me how strange that was. Judging by how few pictures there were of just one twin, I could see now why I hadn't. They were together always. As babies in their pram; as toddlers, tiny little things with bent legs, holding the hands of a man in shorts and blazer with a pipe in his mouth, who would have been my grandfather, before he went bald; as small children playing on swings; as older ones in new school uniforms. They were not only always together, but always, by the look of it, dressed the same way, whether in smocked dresses or school skirts, in kilts or shorts or trousers.

They were both very thin in those days; they both had long dark hair, tied back in plaits or held in place with barrettes. Although they were very alike, you could always tell them apart. One's face was slightly rounder. The other had a bigger mouth. One was usually smiling — the other usually wasn't.

All the days my mother had been taking us out, she too had been taking photographs. "Smile," she would say each time. "smile," and sometimes I had managed to. I don't know whether Will had. What had those two girls been thinking when they smiled and didn't smile? You couldn't tell, any more than anyone would ever be able to tell what Will or I had been thinking, up at Castleton, outside the Tram Museum, alongside the stepped waterfalls at Chatsworth. That was the past now too, as this was the past — my mother's. A time when I hadn't been thought of or Will, from which we were shut out, just as people in the future would be shut out from our smiles, or lack of them, in the photos taken of us.

In all this time while we were looking through the first album, the blue one, Will didn't say a word, nor did I. He never even asked which of the two girls was his mother. In respect for his grief — maybe I was afraid of it — nor did I, though I wanted to. Meanwhile I assumed the little girl with the round face was likely to be my mother. My grown-up mother had gone inside now, as if she didn't want us asking questions and wasn't going to tell us what to think or feel about what we saw. For once I almost wished she would.

We had finished looking through the blue album. At the beginning there had been a note. *June 1948*, it read; (that was when my mother — and Megan, I mustn't forget Megan — had been born.) *June 1948 – June 1958*. Every picture was labeled in the same handwriting and pen, as if they had all been stuck in at the same time.

Maybe they had been hidden away in envelopes and drawers till then, as my mother's pictures of me were. Why had she never gotten round to sticking me in any albums? I thought to myself crossly. Wasn't I worth it? After all, I was her only daughter.

The next book, though, said *July 1961*. There wasn't an end. It wasn't even full, Will opened the wrong end first and the final pages were blank.

On the first page there was a big photograph by itself, which looked as if it had been taken in a studio. One of the twins was standing by the other, her hand on the back of the chair in which she sat.

It was a color photograph, and the twins as usual wore the same dress; blue velvet this time, with puffed sleeves and even sashes, the sort of thing I wouldn't have been seen dead in, and was surprised they would, weren't people all Beatles fans by then, or hippies?

Well, that was one thing. The other was that in this photograph the two of them looked quite different. You could easily tell them apart. The twin standing up was much fatter than the other. Also she was smiling; she looked jolly and happy. Her sister, on the other hand, was thin and pale. She wasn't smiling at all; she looked quite miserable.

Having no evidence to the contrary, I know which one I assumed was my mother. Will assumed the same, and he ought to have known better than me — after all, he had seen both sisters, which was more than I had.

My mother had come back without us hearing her. Will still hadn't asked anything; he was about to turn the page when she leaned over and said, "Oh, those awful blue dresses. Mine was always too big on me and Meg's was always too small."

I looked at her in amazement, forgetting my almost vow of silence. So did Will, I noticed.

"Your dress was too big?" I exclaimed. "But you were the fat one, not her."

"No, I wasn't. I was thin until I had you. Megan was always the fat one, till she decided to stop eating."

"What do you mean she decided to stop eating? Do you mean she had anorexia nervosa?" I asked, remembering a girl at my old school who had stopped eating and had to leave. Anorexia nervosa was what she'd had. Even though everyone said how awful it was, and how ill she'd become, I'd envied her rather. (I wish *I* could stop eating. I wish even looking at food made *me* feel nauseous. No such luck.)

My mother didn't answer. Will didn't seem to be listening. He was touching the fat girl in the photograph. He was looking and looking. "That's her?" he was asking. "That was really her? My mum?" The first time he'd said *mum* since he'd been here. And then he looked as if he wished he hadn't said it. He took a Jaffa cake from the tea tray and stuffed it into his mouth, hardly seeming to know what he was doing, as if the taste of chocolate and marmalade was a terrible shock to him when he caught it.

# 4

## W I L L

Twice in those first few days my cousin Becky looked at me like I was some kind of nutcase. (And so I am, in a way; they don't send you to all those psychologists for nothing. It's called being deprived. Not to mention being a bloody nuisance.)

The first time was when I asked her if she had a little brother. The second time was in that cave when the kid started screaming. The fact was I'd been trying to persuade myself for three whole days that I hadn't really heard the kid yelling the night I arrived. I'd almost succeeded, had almost begun to believe I'd just imagined the whole thing. But as soon as the wailing started up in the cave I knew I hadn't imagined it. It seemed to me, what's more, that the first kid had set off the second on purpose, just to remind me, to make sure I knew that he was real. Don't tell me why he did, let alone how he could have. But that's how it seemed to me.

You can't escape me, he could have been saying. And sure enough, that very night I heard him again in my bedroom, and again, of course, he gave me the creeps. All the same it wasn't quite so much of a shock. In a funny sort of way I had been expecting it. I even fell asleep with the crying still going on, though it took quite a long time. This was not to say that I liked it. Next night, though I knew quite well by now that Soldier and Sailor wasn't supposed to be upstairs at night, that it was an accident one of them had gotten out once and sneaked his way to my room, I crept down to the kitchen as soon as it was dark and lugged one upstairs by the collar.

Soldier or Sailor — I still couldn't tell them apart — didn't lie on my feet this time; he put his head on the pillow alongside mine. He even licked up the tears that I couldn't altogether stop from coming after seeing those pictures of my mum. When the crying woke me again I good as found my hand buried in his fur.

But it wasn't just crying I heard, neither, not that night. There was words somewhere, like the kid was trying to say something to me and no one else, only it wasn't nothing I could understand — nor did I want to understand it.

Maybe the dog understood, though. He seemed to hear the crying, certain. He was whining very softly, whimpering, shivering even; licking my face as if to comfort himself at the same time as trying to comfort me. But in the morning he was gone. Maybe I took him back down, I don't remember. Anyone would think I had gone down, though, seeing what we found later.

I'd never had to decide before whether I believed in

ghosts. But now I was beginning to think I did believe in them. If it wasn't a ghost, that voice I kept hearing, what was it? Much more impossible things happened in science fiction, after all. In fact more impossible things happened in science; things scientists used to say wasn't so, mostly because they couldn't work out how they could be. Maybe, in due course, scientists would prove ghosts and explain them. Thinking about that voice I even hoped that they would. To me, something science could explain wasn't half as scary as something it didn't know how to.

All I knew about ghosts, though, in the meantime, was that they usually belonged to a person who'd once lived in the place they insisted on haunting; in other words, the kid I heard crying had most likely lived in this very house.

At breakfast next morning, casual like, I asked Becky when her house was likely to have been built. She looked at me as if I must be crazy to ask her, and said, in her Derbyshire accent that reminds me of Mum a bit, only more so, "How should I know? Well, I do know it wasn't always just one house, but three cottages knocked together. That's why the stairs are so narrow and awkward and the upstairs rooms so tiny. Why don't you ask Mum about it?"

The trouble with asking Aunt Maggie anything, though, was that you tended to get more information than you bargained for. Even if it was only her way of trying to make me feel at home, it didn't. Not only I still didn't feel at home, I was beginning to get the feeling I never would. In fact I'd almost made up my mind that I wouldn't stay on here after the holidays. It was my own choice, after all; Ms. Simms had said so. (Becky, I thought, would be glad to see the back of me; I didn't know so much about Aunt Maggie. But it wasn't up to none of them.)

So that morning, instead of throwing questions at Aunt Maggie, I went for a walk with Becky — she must be short of friends, I thought, if she wanted to go traipsing round with me, that made two of us had nothing better to do. All the time we was walking I looked round for the village I was supposed to be living in, that I hadn't seen no sign of till now.

"There's a post office," Becky said, looking across at the little pointed green hills set against each other here and there, without no order to them. "Well, sort of; someone just has it in her front room a few hours a day, to help folks out is why she says she does it. There isn't a pub. If there was a pub, there might be a disco. Well, there might be." (But she didn't sound hopeful.)

"Isn't there no shops then?" I asked. "If there's a post office?"

"*Shops*? You must be joking. You can't buy so much as a button or a packet of cornflakes in this place. It's a village and not a village, *this* place." (She said "a village and not a village," as you might say "somewhere and nowhere." As far as I was concerned it about summed up the way I felt.)

Looking around us, I could see she wasn't pulling a fast one. Apart from the little green hills and houses in the distance across the far side of the valley, there wasn't nothing to be seen except farms and fields and sheep plus a few cows in more colors than I knew cows came in: black-and-white cows, for instance, white ones, black ones, and red ones. There was red berries on some small trees. There was tall purple flowers along the hedgerows. Where the flower heads was dying they left little fat, pale spikes, some of them shedding stuff that looked like cotton. I knew those flowers' name. I'd seen them in London, along the underground.

"That's rosebay willow herb," my mother had told me a few times. "That's your flower, Will." Which is how I remember the name so well; in fact how could I forget it? "If I ever have a sister are you going to call her Rose?" I used to ask. Why did I keep seeing things this morning that reminded me of Mum? I wondered, as we passed a man in a tractor cutting grass in a great swath behind him, at the same time throwing up dust that made me sneeze.

"Do you have hay fever?" Becky asked.

"How should I know," I said. "I ain't never seen no hay till now."

In the next field Becky waved her hand at some humpy bits ringed by a broken fence. "That's an old mine," she said. "The fence is to stop you going any closer. People are always falling down old mines and potholes round here. Sometimes they never come out. Someone didn't come out of this mine once, they say," she added ghoulishly, as if she liked the idea of it. I didn't.

"Maybe there was miners living in your house," I said, "when it was just cottages."

"Like I said," answered Becky in a bored voice, "why don't you ask Mum?"

We hadn't had no proper walk, more of a meander really. After less than an hour we was back looking down at the house already, with its narrow little windows, and inside, unseen, its narrower little stairs, which had the big cupboard standing at the top. "How do you get the furniture upstairs, then?" I asked Becky, curiously. "Through the windows? You'd never get beds and suchlike up those stairs, would you?"

But I knew it was a stupid question even as I asked it, and the worst of it was that once again it reminded me of Mum. "Through windows that size, you must be joking," Becky was saying, waving at them scornfully. Before I could stop myself I burst out, "Mum and I saw a grand piano go in a house through the windows once, dangling on a kind of crane. Mum said it needed a Charlie Chaplin sitting playing it at the same time." (But why was I talking about Mum? I wondered. I didn't

56

want to talk about Mum to no one, least of all to Becky.)

"Tell me about your mother, Will. What was she like? Didn't she ever get fat again?" asked Becky. But if she thought I was going to tell her — even if I had given her the excuse to ask, even if I could have told her — she had another think coming.

"Mind your own business," I muttered, kicking the road.

Becky didn't give up, though; I'd noticed she didn't tend to give up nothing easily.

"It is my business. She was my aunt as well as your mother."

"So what?" I pushed her this time. I only just managed not to kick her as well. Then I ran ahead of her down the hill, up to my room, and flung myself onto the bed. I pummeled and pummeled it, I was so angry; I would have smashed the glass on the rose pictures if I had dared. I did heave all the bedding off the bed after a bit and throw my things here, there, everywhere. I threw Isaac Asimov out of the window and immediately wished I hadn't. How dare she, how dare she, I was yelling inside my head. Any moment she'll be asking me about my dad too. How dare she what? I wondered after a while, starting to pick everything up again because no one else was going to.

I calmed down after a while. I even laughed at the

memory of Becky's face when I pushed her. Lying on my back, staring up at the sloping ceiling, it occurred to me that this would have been the only bedroom in this house when it was a single cottage, that a whole lot of people must have slept together once in the room I now had to myself. How come there's not a whole nursery load of kids keeping me awake, instead of just the one? I wondered. The way I was feeling, I wasn't inclined to be grateful for such small mercies. Still I had too many questions now. I couldn't not ask them no longer. At lunch, over bread and cheese and pickle, I at last stuck my neck out and got round to asking Aunt Maggie a few.

"Who were the people who lived here? Oh, they'd've worked for the Big House," she told us. "Or for the farm belonging to the Big House, or the quarry at the cliff face down at the bottom of the park, or in the woods."

"Or the mine?" I asked her.

"Or maybe the mine. I'm not sure who the mine belonged to."

"And all for nothing," said Becky, who had been scowling at me forever. (I scowled back at her, or made silly faces. She didn't seem to care about either.) "Mr. Peters, the history teacher at school, said that in those days rich people made poor people work for near nothing."

"Speak for yourself. *I'm* a poor person," I said,

making another face at her, a poor person's face. At the same time I made my knife squeak against my plate until she and her mum both started complaining that I was setting their teeth on edge. (I used to drive all my foster mothers mad in such ways. Maybe they'd rather I'd lain on the floor and kicked my heels and screamed, like I'd seen other kids doing. But who was I to make their lives easier? I'd think. I used to put frogs in their cake tins and watch the women scream when the frogs jumped out. If Becky wasn't careful, I thought, I'd put a frog in her bed.)

Becky got worse than frogs, though, that very evening, after dinner, after we'd carried the coffee tray into the sitting room the way we always did. (The coffee was for Aunt Maggie and Uncle Jim, of course, and not for us. It was too near bedtime for us to drink coffee, they said. Becky grumbled about it every night.) Not that what Becky found in the sitting room was any doing of mine, so far as I knew, unless I'd taken to walking in my sleep. It was hard enough to keep track of myself in the day, I thought. I couldn't be answerable for my dreams also, let alone my sleep.

The sitting room was the biggest room in the house; in fact it was two rooms made into one, Aunt Maggie said. It was still low-ceilinged, though, with three big black beams holding it up. The back window was the one on the road so low you could have kicked it in from there, if you wanted. But you couldn't have kicked it in from here. The ground at the back of the house was lower than at the front, so the window was set in the wall waist-high, that is, ordinary level. The chairs and sofa was deep and soft. The green carpet felt lush as grass, too lush if you ask me. It was like it hadn't never been walked on, like it didn't belong to no one.

The two big albums, the red and the blue one, lay on the same low table in front of the empty fireplace that we set the coffee tray down on. Becky knelt down on the carpet, beside it, then took up the second album, the red one. Two scraps of white card fell out of it onto the floor — I didn't think nothing of that at first and nor did she seem to. It was only when I turned one piece over and found it was shiny and dark on the other side that I realized where they came from. At the same moment my cousin flung open the album at the first page to find countless more pieces of the big studio photo of our mothers in their blue velvet dresses. Some of the bits had been stuck back on the empty page they'd been torn from in the first place, but all mixed up like an undone jigsaw. In the middle, side by side, was set a smiling mouth and a scowling mouth minus the rest of their faces; you couldn't tell which twin owned smile or frown no longer.

Even if my mum was dead and she didn't have a mouth no more, Becky's mum still had one, I thought. Was hers the same mouth as the scowling one in the picture? I mean, did any of the same tissue and skin remain or had it all been replaced over the years? Had Aunt Maggie, bit by bit, without no one seeing, grown a new mouth? I wondered.

Looking up at her, I saw that her mouth, old mouth or new one, wasn't scowling now, or smiling. It was open. Two arms had shot out from the shoulders below it, two hands grabbed Becky's shoulders, hauled her to her feet, and started shaking her, violently, the way Becky had deserved shaking all these days, but maybe didn't deserve to be shaken just now. Meanwhile screams started coming out of those two angry lips that my mum might have known once, or not as the case may be.

"Mum, Mum. It wasn't me, I didn't," I heard Becky wailing. She was telling the truth to my mind. She hadn't torn the picture up, don't tell me how I knew, unless it was that her voice sounded different from the one I'd mostly heard her speaking in. It was just a girl's voice really, and frightened. Anyone might be frightened at the sight of their mum going berserk. I could have felt sorry for her, I almost did. But then I didn't. Because any moment Aunt Maggie might get the message and turn on me instead, and who knows but she might have been right to turn on me. Like I said, who knows what I was doing in my sleep — not me, for starters. Meantime, Becky was getting the worst of it, flailing away uselessly at her mother with her hands and all the while being shaken, like a dog might be shaken.

It wasn't me pulled them apart, neither, though maybe it should have been. Watching them in a mixture of glee and mortal terror, I didn't move one single inch, not even when Becky's dad, Uncle Jim, walked into the room carrying his spectacles and paper. At that very moment Becky was pushed so hard against the little table that the coffee slopped all over it, staining the lush green carpet. It was a wonder the whole thing didn't go flying — it did, very nearly.

I don't know what Uncle Jim was thinking. A fat man who had been fatter — his trousers was loose on him, he had to keep hitching them up — he looked startled at first, like he didn't expect to find no one going bananas, though how he could have missed that noise from a long way off, I really can't tell you. It was true he did tend to seem distracted most of the time — "thinking about business," Becky said. He'd hardly spoken one single word to me, for instance, since the day I came.

He clued up now, though, quick enough. "That's enough," he bellowed, throwing down his spectacles and paper. "Hasn't there been enough already?" (By "enough" he meant me, I supposed, inasmuch as I wasn't past supposing.) The next moment he'd separated Becky's shoulders from her mother's big red hands and quelled the screams, seemingly, by the same very simple action; the whole business can't have lasted more than a minute from start to finish. As soon as it was over you could even have believed it never happened. Aunt Maggie, though still panting, her breast heaving, her eyes glittering like lasers, was bending down to wipe up the spilled coffee.

I'd got ghosts on the brain, maybe. For an instant, while Aunt Maggie was screaming, I could have sworn I saw a little white face pressed against the back window — the one so low to the road you'd think any body belonging to any such face must be stood deep down in the earth to get there. There was no sign of no face next time I dared to look. I doubted already if I'd seen it in the first place.

I didn't doubt the crying I heard in the night, though, not any longer. No more did I doubt the words I heard it saying to me. For there was definite words this time, the same two words, over and over, very plain and simple. But it wasn't no use their being so simple that even I could understand them, either one or both together. There wasn't nothing I could do about them; zero bloody nothing.

"Help me," the voice said. "Help me." Whoever it was. Whatever help it needed.

# 5

## BECKY

When I think of it I've seen Mum maddened often enough. But I've never seen her go absolutely crazy. I never even knew she could go absolutely crazy. It was another thing I didn't know about her. It felt a bit like seeing the hill opposite our house, the one I always took for granted, falling down in a second. I almost hated my mother because I couldn't take her for granted anymore, either. Maybe I should have hated Will's mother, Megan, instead, since it was all her fault, not my mother's. The trouble was she was dead, and how can you hate anyone who's dead? Maybe you can, though. Maybe it's safer than hating someone still alive. Or maybe it isn't.

Well, one thing I can say for certain; it wasn't me who tore up that picture, even if I'd wanted to, and I expect in a way I had. It wasn't Dad either, or my mother. That left only Will. But I don't see how it could have been Will. I saw his face. He didn't look like someone who'd expected what we found there. My mother believed it was him, though, as soon as she got over thinking it was her daughter.

Next morning she took me down to the garden before breakfast to pick plums. It was a lovely morning, I remember, one of those late summer ones, before the chestnuts are quite ripe. There was dew on the grass and wasp-eaten plums under our feet. Reaching up to pick, she kept her back turned, not turning round to look at me once until she'd quite finished apologizing for losing her temper that evening. I wished she wouldn't. She didn't have to, I thought. Though there had been other times when I'd felt my mother owed me an apology for something she had said or done, now that an apology was forthcoming it made me more unhappy than anything; it felt quite wrong, really. (Anyway, how can you apologize for turning into a mad woman? For making your daughter think the world's gone crazy? That nothing is certain anymore? That a hill fell down that should have stood upright forever?)

Afterward — she did turn round and look at me then — she made me promise I'd been telling her the truth when I said I hadn't torn up the photograph in the red album. I picked plums too, meanwhile, but very slowly. And I didn't put mine into her bowl, as I was supposed to. As soon as I had a handful I ate them, one by one, listening to her telling me how Will must still be so grieving for his mother, he couldn't have known what he was doing.

"You mean you think he did it?" I asked her.

"Who else could it have been?" she said. "You must try and be extra nice to him, Becky." She had turned round from her plum tree again, to look at me. But I was staring at the fine purple dust on a plum I was about to eat, gently rubbing it off a bit at a time, until the skin turned darker and shinier. "If anything further happens I'll get on to a doctor about him. Or that nice social worker who said call her anytime. Don't you think that would be a good idea, Becky?"

And that was another peculiar thing. My mother didn't usually ask for my advice. Not that there had ever been such a problem in our house before, but even so it was peculiar.

"You could do," I said. "If he stays. But you don't even know if he will stay yet, do you?"

"Has he said anything to you about that, duck?"

"Not really," I said, awkwardly. It felt somehow disloyal suddenly, talking about Will like this to my mother. He was the same age as me, after all, and my cousin, even if he didn't look it. Blood is thicker than water, I nearly reminded my mother, but thought better of it. "I'm not sure he likes it much here," I said reluctantly. "So maybe he won't stay."

Up till then, I'd been longing for him to go. But in the moment of saying it, I wasn't so sure after all. Of course, I still didn't think I liked him. On the other hand I didn't have another cousin. On the other hand if it wasn't Will who tore up the photograph, or me, who was it? Wasn't there something funny going on in our house? Nothing so funny had ever happened before Will turned up, at least nothing quite of this sort.

There was a big bowl of plums on the breakfast table. Will shook his head when I offered him one; he even made a face. Fancy not liking that delicious yellow flesh, its sweet juice oozing over your tongue; as my mother says, there's no accounting for taste. He seemed cheerful enough, though, not at all like someone "in a state of grief and shock" the way Mum had described him. When Mum gave us a list of places she could take us to that morning — I suppose she was trying to make up for her behavior the night before — he chipped in before I'd time to open my mouth and said where he really wanted to go was the Mining Museum at Matlock Bath.

Actually if my mother hadn't tried to push it down my throat so often, I might be quite interested in the mining round here myself. I might be quite interested in a lot of things — in Arkwright's Mill, for instance, the first cotton mill in the country. They took us round that from my old school and it was really interesting once they had explained all about it.

But if I'd told my mother she would have thrown a ton of books at me, not to mention giving ten history lessons. Why bother? And now it's occurred to me to wonder if she'd always been like that, if she'd driven Megan mad when they were little by going on and on about the things she was interested in, or that Megan was interested in, or at least had been before my mother homed relentlessly in on her.

I didn't say any of this to Will, of course. Blood may be thicker than water, after all. (Unfortunately, though, when it's him.)

The Mining Museum is a very gloomy museum, which is appropriate I suppose, as mines and caves are gloomy. The floors were wooden and echoed under our feet, and the walls were very dark. There were glass cases full of bits of different-colored rock, all of them coming from around these parts, as if anyone needed reminding that we live in a rocky country.

I know that the rock the Dales are made of — and the cliffs above our head at Matlock Bath — is called limestone and that it's light gray in color, not like the millstone grit just down the road, which is redder and darker. I also know (I learned this on school field trips — it's called "getting to know your environment") that limestone is a hard rock but can be dissolved by water. This is why it's full of caves, carved out by streams and springs and so forth. It's also full of different kinds of metals, not just lead, even though there used to be more lead mines than anything. All of this seemed to interest Will more than it interested me, judging by the time he spent looking at the explanations and pictures. He also seemed to like the descriptions of the mines themselves, how they worked, also the names of the different kinds of veins and things; rakes and scrins and flats and pipes — maybe I would have bothered to find out what they were myself if he hadn't been so interested.

He stood peering for hours at glass cases full of rusty tools with names like bucking iron and cobbing hammer, gad and wedge, nogger and kibble. I liked the names, but trying to work out what they were all for made my head ache. The big iron pin men arranged to show how miners worked with some of those tools didn't help in the slightest. They looked so unreal and yet so lifelike, the pin men, they upset me — I imagined them coming to life in the museum at night and running wild all over it.

The models of the pumps they used to pump water out of the shafts were equally baffling. Will was getting as bad as my mother, I thought sourly, seeing how interested he was. Water was one problem, he explained; when you got so far down in the rock you met water, you had to pump it out before you could start hammering away at the metals.

"Don't teach your grandmother to suck eggs," I warned him. But actually all I could think about were those caves and tunnels we'd seen already, and how horrible it must have been to spend your days in the dark and the wet, hammering away at rock. I also thought about the boy they said you could hear crying.

I hadn't heard him, luckily. So he couldn't have gotten stuck down our mine, the one Will and I had passed. I rather hoped he hadn't. That would be a bit too close to home for comfort.

Meantime Will, yet again, was talking about getting to the center of the earth.

"I'd rather get to the stars, myself," I said, "talking of mysterious and unreachable places." (But I only said it for the sake of saying it. I wouldn't really have wanted to go there, either.)

"Stars are only lumps of rock," said Will. "What's the difference? Apart from stars being farther." Meanwhile I looked at the pictures of the boys and the women in bonnets who worked up on the surface crushing the rock to get the iron ore out and was glad it wasn't me having to do that kind of work for a living. Did the women work like that in the mine near us? I wondered. Did the boys? Did they ever go down into the mine? Or what? Was that how the boy got lost, working in whichever mine it was? Or had he just been playing?

But the boy, whoever he was, wasn't the reason I hated the Mining Museum forever after. The shafts were the reason, the ones you could climb up and down between the two floors of the museum, thereby discovering for yourself how it must have felt climbing up and down mine shafts. They were very narrow mine shafts. They must have been pretty thin people.

"How about you?" my mother urged Will and me. "Why don't you two have a go?"

Will went first. He was all right, of course, being so thin, not to say skinny. And though I didn't like the look of those narrow tunnels, I wasn't going to be outdone. I followed straight after. At least I started to follow him. But I got no farther than the bottom of the shaft at first and just stood there, my head in the opening, peering up at Will's ascending blue sneakers.

"Go on, Becky," encouraged my mother.

"How about you trying then?" I said nastily, eyeing her bulk.

Will shouted down. "The problem is Becky thinks she's too fat, she's going to get stuck. They're very narrow those places, ain't they, Becky?"

Well, I wasn't having that — how dare he call me fat; shouting it loud enough, what's more, for everyone to hear him. To make matters worse, my mother said suddenly, "Well, if Becky won't try, maybe I will."

I looked at her in horror. She couldn't be serious. She wouldn't even get into the shaft, I thought, let alone up it. She'd make herself a laughingstock in front of all the people. (The museum was quite full now, with women and children mainly; other mothers trying to amuse their children toward the end of the long holidays, I dare say, just as my mother was doing.)

Did those children ever pity their mothers? I wondered. Being embarrassed was normal. My mother had embarrassed me for as long as I could remember. But *pity?* That was something altogether different. Yet I did pity her suddenly, her knowing she'd never make it but pretending she could though.

"Of course I'm not too fat," I said, eyeing, rather sadly, her big bosom swelling under the faded checked shirt. "I'll show you."

I dare say what happened thereafter was funny for anyone else watching. Things like that always are funny if it doesn't happen to be you who's suffering. But I didn't think it funny either then or later. I made a fool of myself, and in public too, and it was all Will's and my mother's fault, I decided. (Not that Will, at least, didn't get his comeuppance, and serve him right, I considered. I mean, he looked as if he had seen a ghost for the second time since I'd known him.)

It was all right climbing the shaft at first. I bent down and crept into the bottom of it, reached up, held on to some iron pegs, and pulled myself up onto more pegs, set for my feet. Though it was narrow enough, I could manage it. And pretty soon I could see the hole at the top I had to come out of, into the top floor of the museum. What's the problem, I was thinking, what's the problem? This isn't a real mine. This is a cinch.

But then the shaft got narrower. And then suddenly it wasn't all right. I couldn't move an inch; at least I couldn't get up any farther. That didn't alarm me too much at the beginning, though it annoyed me;

I could always go backward, I thought, if worse came to worst. But when, very crossly, I reached one foot down to the peg below the one I was standing on, I found I couldn't reach that one either, no matter that I wriggled and wriggled until my chest and shoulders and bottom seemed to be swelling up by the minute.

At first I was too busy trying to free myself to realize how scared I was. And then for a few minutes longer, I was too angry to feel my fear, seeing Will's face peering down at me.

"What's the matter then?" he asked. "Got stuck then, fatty?" And he was laughing.

In my rage I gave another almighty heave. My shoulders and bosom went upward and my feet found the next peg.

"Of course I'm not stuck," I said, triumphantly. And I pushed on up again. But this time it was useless. This time I was stuck — hopelessly, entirely.

I could hear my mother behind me — I couldn't see her, of course — asking, "Are you all right, Becky?" I could see Will's grinning face. Behind him I could see other faces: a little boy in a red T-shirt, a woman with long, blond hair. They were all laughing, or so it seemed to me as I struggled and struggled, and bit by bit I wasn't angry anymore. I was frightened. It's not nice having your body caught fast from knees to shoulders, scraping and grinding in a narrow shaft, nothing to hold on to but iron pegs and railings. You start thinking you'll be stuck in your little dark space forever. After a while I even lost the desire to reach up and clock Will one for laughing at me. All I wanted was to get out, but I couldn't.

I burst into tears. "Help me," I said, looking up at Will's face, which seemed now to fill the whole space above me. "Help me."

I don't know what happened then. He didn't help me — that was certain. But I felt someone or something pulling at my feet, and what with that and the white, sudden terror I saw in his face, it was enough to dislodge me. No longer wanting or trying to reach the top of the shaft anymore, I let myself be pulled back downward, watching Will's face above me all the while growing ever more distant. "Help me," I kept saying, not because I needed his help any longer but because I wanted to see what it did to him. "Help me. Why won't you help me?"

And then I was free, crouched at the bottom of the shaft, wiping away my tears, determined not to come out into the open, to reveal myself, until I'd grown calmer. Until I could look and behave as if nothing had happened.

"Well, well," I said, as jauntily as I could when I emerged finally, brushing myself down. "That's a tight fit. It's really only meant for kids. Just as well you didn't have a go, Mother." I was staring all round me meanwhile, daring anyone to laugh. Luckily the kids still waiting were too eager to try the climb themselves to be that much interested in me now that I'd freed myself.

"I wasn't really stuck," I said. "I'd had enough, that's all. It's pretty claustrophobic. Who'd want to work in a real mine? Sooner them than me."

How about being stuck like that a hundred feet down? I was thinking, determined never to risk any such thing. (Or to eat another Mars bar, for that matter.) What help would there have been for me a hundred feet down? Or even fifty?)

There was no sign of Will. We waited for him to come down and find us, but he didn't. After ten minutes Mum sent me up to look. I couldn't see him anywhere at first. I was beginning to think he must have gone back down one of the shafts and we'd missed him, when suddenly I noticed a boy standing in a corner, behind a big case full of tools, his face to the glass, his hands spread flat like starfish. Who else but Will, of course. The second time I called him he turned his head and I saw that his eyes were closed. Even when he opened his eyes he kept staring so blindly it was as if he couldn't see me, any more than he could have seen those tools in front of him.

I forgot he had laughed at me now. I felt alarmed seeing him like that, like someone as far away as space or farther. His face was white as paper.

"It's all right, Will," I said. "I'm out. I wasn't

really stuck. It wasn't a real mine, after all, nothing much could have happened to me. And anyway you were laughing. Why did you find it so funny?"

"Funny?" he said then. "It wasn't funny."

"Why were you laughing at me then?"

"I wasn't laughing."

"Come down, Will. Mum says we can try the cable car again, if we like, before the queue builds up again."

"Cable car — I don't want to go in no cable car," he said; to prove it he was sick in the gutter as soon as we got outside. My mother drove us home then and put him to bed for the rest of the morning. That was the second time we didn't go on the cable car, although it was one of the things I really liked, that we went on most holidays. We even had a season ticket.

# 6

## WILL

Even though I'm not a camel, that "Help me. Help me," was the last straw. I good as got on the train to London straight off, soon as I'd finished throwing up. The voice was persecuting me, I tell you. Putting itself in where it shouldn't have been; where it couldn't have been, looked at logically. First it had sounded from a kid with a Snoopy T-shirt screaming in a cave, then from my fat cousin Becky stuck in the shaft in the Mining Museum. "Help me. Help me." Her voice and not her voice. But if not hers, whose was it? Someone else who got stuck in the ground once? Or what?

I told Aunt Maggie next morning I'd made up my mind I didn't want to stay on in Derbyshire. I'd rather go back to school in London.

"Oh, dear, why not? Are you still not feeling well? Don't you like it here?" she asked in a worried voice, as if it mattered.

"It's all right," I said. "It ain't that."

"Well, if you do like it, what is it, Will? We would be so pleased if you did decide to stay on with us and go to the school with Becky. Of course we know it must

77

be strange for you up here, after living all your life in London."

"It ain't that, neither," I answered.

"Then what is it, Will? Maybe we can do something about it."

Squatting down in front of the stove between Soldier and Sailor — it had been chillier these last two mornings — I tried to explain, but it wasn't no good trying to. There wasn't nothing I could say that didn't sound like I hated the place. But that wasn't the point exactly, wasn't what I wanted to say.

I made such a hash of explaining, I got myself so tangled up, that after a few minutes I heard myself promising to stay for another two or three days at least, to give her time to talk to Ms. Simms and so on. Then she left me alone in the kitchen still stroking Soldier and Sailor, feeling almost sorry by then that I wouldn't be staying for more than those two or three days I'd promised.

For what did I have to go back to really? Also I'd miss the dogs, I thought. They seemed to like me all right, even if Becky didn't. One of them had taken to following me upstairs to bed each night. Though he was always fetched back by one of Becky's parents, I'd go and get him later; by this time he'd taken to waiting for me by the door and would thump his tail quietly as soon as I came in.

That was Soldier, I think — I'd begun to tell the two

apart now, more or less. He was a bit taller than Sailor. His fur was a bit yellower and longer. His tail had burrs stuck all down it, which each night I tried to unpick.

I don't suppose Becky was sorry when I told her I was going. In fact, she smiled. But then, straightaway, she offered to lend me her Walkman, which she never had before, so maybe in a way she was sorry. Or else, more likely, it was a guilty conscience; she hadn't tried to make me feel at home exactly, had she? The opposite in fact.

Aunt Maggie cooked sausages for lunch and for once I felt hungry. I ate three, and a load of oven chips, and most of a bottle of ketchup on them. It was strange, I thought, it was like deciding to go back to London had somehow made me feel at home. I half found myself regretting that I was going. Now it came to it, I wondered if I wanted to leave Derbyshire at all.

In the afternoon, accepting Becky's loan of her Walkman I went into the garden to read. I'd finished the Asimov I'd rescued from the garden the day I threw it out. Now I was reading a story about extraterrestrial beings disguised as men and trying to colonize the earth, meeting their match when they came across other extraterrestrial beings disguised as men.

Perhaps I'm an extraterrestrial being, I thought — I felt like one sometimes, that was true. Perhaps Becky and her family is extraterrestrial beings. Perhaps I'd suspected her and she'd suspected me of not being properly human all along. Perhaps the only thing we hadn't managed to work out properly was which of us was the superior being; which of us would in the end outwit — outgun — the other. It was nice of her to lend me her Walkman, of course. But it wasn't nice of her not to have lent it to me sooner.

In fact, while I was thinking out all this it seemed to me suddenly that she really had begun playing extraterrestrial tricks, or rather that her Walkman had, which came to the same thing. I was listening to one of her old Beatles tapes at the time, lying in the place under the apple tree by the swing I'd come to like best in the whole garden, and reading about the extraterrestrial sheriff who believed he was keeping a whole lot of human beings in order, only they wasn't human. And he wasn't keeping them in order at all, really. I'd gotten so interested in it I'd almost forgotten about the Beatles, despite their thump and yell in my eardrums. I only remembered they was there, in fact, when another noise crept in among them; a noise without a beat. A yell that didn't have no rhythm. A muttering that wasn't like music.

As soon as I caught it, I knew it for what it was. "Help me," was one set of words, but there was others I couldn't follow. There was cries too, and wailings; small sounds compared with the music, but you couldn't mistake them. In a little while, to my ears, they'd almost drowned out the music.

The way I jumped and yelled, you'd have thought one of the wasps buzzing around had stung me. But they hadn't. These wasps kept their distance, like they didn't fancy what I was hearing neither, exactly the same kinds of noise as invaded me night after night. After a minute or two I couldn't bear it no longer. I pulled the Walkman off my head and flung it against the apple tree, headphones, wires, and all.

This wasn't, of course, the best moment for Becky to turn up, but being Becky, of course, she did. I turned round to find her standing transfixed, with her mouth open, just outside the sitting-room door. She didn't stay transfixed for long, though. I'd never have guessed she knew how to move so fast. She hurtled down the garden, picked up the little black box, its wires and headphones trailing, plonked the headphones on her head, listened for a moment, fiddled with it, then screeched out, "You bloody little . . . THING . . . You've broken my Walkman."

Then she launched herself at me. That was another thing I'd never've expected. I didn't have no time to get out of the way, and as for stopping her, she was twice as big as I was. In a moment we was rolling round and round under the apple tree, thrashing out at each other the way we'd both been wanting to thrash out at each other since the day I came; if she wasn't glad of the excuse, then I was. The only problem was I didn't like to hit her too hard, not least she could have given me much worse, easy, being the size she was. As it was she ended sitting on top of me, squashing me flat it felt like. When I opened my eyes and stared up at her I saw that she was crying. "Why did you?" she was yelling, between sobs, leaning down to shake my helpless shoulders. "Why did you break it? It wasn't as if I ever wanted you here in the first place."

"Nor I didn't never want to come here in the first place," I said as well as I could, the breath near squashed out of me. I was crying too, or at least my cheeks was wet. "What did you do to it? What did you put on the tape?" I begged her.

She stopped shaking me; looked down at me blankly. "Put on the tape? What do you mean?"

"Noises," I pleaded. "Voices. Over the music. You know."

But she didn't know. Of course she hadn't put nothing on it. I knew before I said it; before I even saw that look in her eyes again, like she thought I was crazy. I suppose I should have been used to that look by now, but I wasn't. At least, though, it drove out her rage; she sat quite still for a bit, thoughtful, avoiding my eyes. At last she hauled herself off me as she might have hauled herself off a cushion she'd happened to land on, then gathered up her broken Walkman and left, shaking her head, not allowing me one more word.

That night, after I'd said good night and gone upstairs, I didn't climb straight into my bed. First I packed up my worldly goods in the red zipper bag, then I sat in the windowsill reading the story about the extraterrestrial beings until it was time to fetch Soldier upstairs. I wasn't going to spend another night in this room without him. After tonight I didn't mean to spend another night in this room at all. Tomorrow, without waiting to tell no one, I would lug my red zipper bag out of the front door and walk down the hill to catch the little train to Derby. From Derby I would catch a train to London, and in London I'd catch the tube and go straight to Ms. Simms' office. That was that.

Meanwhile, as soon as it was dark and I had Soldier safely under my arm in bed, I put out my hand to turn the light off. Held it for a minute, looking at the room almost regretfully. For though it still didn't look like no room of mine, with its buttercup and daisy patterns and pictures of roses, I was used to it by now, just as I was used to the racket of the flaming rooks outside fussing about in the treetops. I'd even gotten to like the rooks, I'd miss them, I thought. It wasn't no big black birds gave me the creeps, nor the room, it was just a room. I looked round it one more time. Then I turned the light off. And waited.

It was quite a little wail I heard first. Maybe no one but me what was expecting it would have noticed. But then came little whispering words, like a question more than a statement, almost an apology, in fact. "Help me?" I heard. And again. "Help me?" All spoke in a tone wretched enough to shift the hardest heart, except mine was harder, so I thought, as I answered it back for the first time, also the last if things went the way I intended. "No way. No way. How can I?"

"Help me."

"How can I help no one dead for I don't know how long?"

"Help me."

"And anyway from now on I won't be here to help you." This was my final argument; my last word, against which it couldn't say nothing, could it? I mean it couldn't follow me. Could it? Well, I'd make sure that it couldn't.

"HELP ME."

"I'm leaving tomorrow. I won't hear one more squeak out of you, not never."

Intending to banish the voice for good and all — in this room it'd never yet spoken except when it was dark — I put out a hand to turn on the light I'd just switched off. Light in my eyes all night would disturb my sleep much less, I thought, than screams and wailings and pleas for help I couldn't see no way to satisfying. I pushed the switch firmly. Light flashed for a moment, only to be followed by instant and blinding darkness. The bulb exploded.

Soldier had been very tense all this time; my hand so close against him, I noticed he'd been shivering a little, not quite whining. As soon as the bulb blew to smithereens, he gave a yelp and a jump, leaped off the bed and out the door before I could catch him, and fled down the passage howling. Outside the window another great rumpus started, like the rooks thought it was daylight or else had been scared out of their wits like Soldier — or like me, come to that. Except that I wasn't moving or yelling. I was frozen to the bed, my mouth open and yet silent, listening to the rooks squalling and gabbling, to the howls dying away in the darkness.

I don't know if I said it, or if the voice said it for me. Either way it was as much like a thought in my head as a saying. "You'll never lose me. I'll still be there with you. Wherever you think of going." Maybe it didn't say nothing. Maybe I didn't neither. Maybe I had just imagined — thought — it.

"Help me." It came more quietly this time. I was scrabbling around meanwhile for pieces of light bulb. I didn't want none of them for my bedfellows — I'd be covered in cuts in the morning.

"Why don't you help me clear this bloody mess you made?" I suggested, assuming, rightly or wrongly, that the light bulb hadn't blown up for nothing. But of course it — he — didn't help me. How could he, no more than I could do what he — it — wanted.

But if it could come after me, I was thinking, if it was actually threatening that it could, there'd be no point going back to London. Out of sheer cussedness, if you like, it made half of me more determined to go than ever. Except for the thought of having to walk all the way to Derby in the dark, I'd have gone that very moment. But supposing it followed me along the road, I thought; suppose I heard its footsteps behind me — what would I see if I turned round? — no, maybe I hadn't that much bottle, maybe I wouldn't go yet, after all. Maybe it would be safer to stay here in my bed, not leave until morning. But leave I would then, for sure, the cussed half of me was saying.

The other half of me, though, couldn't afford to be so certain. If I'd heard right, if I hadn't imagined or made up the threats it was making, I wouldn't be free of him in London neither. In fact, in London he might refuse to let me go, ever. I mightn't have no means, ever, of getting him out of my head. That would be worse, if anything. If that was to be my fate, then I might just as well stay here, in this house, alongside my cousin Becky. Alongside her, here, might be my only hope of working out this wretchedness.

I went to sleep at last, arguing with myself. And woke in the morning, the two halves of me still divided. My head was aching and I felt like I hadn't slept a wink all night, though I must have.

My red zipper bag was sitting where I'd left it on the armchair, I noticed; not that the sight of it, swollen with my things, answered one single question. Noticing pieces of light bulb still strewn over the floor beside the

bed, I got out the other side, dressed slowly, and at
last went down to breakfast, still quite uncertain. One
moment I like saw myself sitting in a railway carriage,
watching the cooling towers go past. The next I fancied
myself nailed down here forever, the little voice in my
ears saying, "Help me. Help me," my cousin Becky
hanging on to her Walkman and scowling at me, just
as she was scowling at me now, across the breakfast
table. Or maybe she was looking unhappy; maybe she
*was* unhappy, if so, that made two of us.

"What was all that racket in the night?" she was
saying to her mother. "The rooks, didn't you hear
them? And one of the dogs howling."

"There wasn't anything. Your father went down to
look," said Aunt Maggie with a shrug. "Maybe there
was a fox around or something."

It was a gloomy morning, gray outside and in, pretty
much the way Becky and I was feeling. There was a
light on over the breakfast table. I gave its bulb an
apprehensive glance — it was a much bigger bulb than
the one in my bedside lamp — then thought no more
of it, until the words came into my head as I was eating
toast and honey. Words as simple as toast and honey,
but much less sweet; my words this time, quite definite.
They said defiantly, I'm going. Today. I'm going.

I shot another apprehensive look at the kindly light
hanging above the table. Obligingly, you could say,
predictably, you could say, coincidentally, you could

say, it blew up that very moment. I saw it blow this time. There was gloom after, but no dark as there'd been last night. The bulb was huge, like I mentioned. There was glass in the butter and glass in the marmalade, glass on everybody's plates, on the toast, in the cornflake packet. Aunt Maggie shrieked. Becky screamed. Soldier and Sailor fled the room. I threw my hostage to fortune, as my Mum would have put it (she was always throwing hostages to fortune; trouble was, fortune always spat them right back at her), and yelled in my head, I'll stay. If I must. Then I passed out cold under the table. Well, I lay down and shut my eyes. I opened them a moment or two later to see Aunt Maggie and Becky gazing down at me in horror. I winked at them — what else could I do? I was as frightened as they was. I was thinking, I'll stay. If you feel *that* strongly about it. But that don't mean to say I'll help you. How can I?

(Even then I didn't know if I was staying for his sake; or because he gave me no option; or because, in a way, he was making me do what I really wanted, if I was honest; going away, in other words, if I was honest, might be what my mother used to call — that was something else she was good at — "cutting off my nose to spite my face.")

Two days later I went down to London to get the rest of my gear and also to see Ms. Simms. She even met me at the station. I'd hardly gotten off the train when she asked me what I was up to, changing my mind so often.

"Two days ago, Will, your aunt rang me to say you didn't want to stay. That you'd decided to come back to London. Now you say you are going to stay. What's with you then? What's up?"

"I didn't change my mind," I said. "I just put it round a different way, that's all. I decided to give it a bit longer."

"That's today, Will. What about tomorrow?"

"Who cares about tomorrow?"

"Thirteen-year-old boys have no business being cynical," she told me. It was one of the things I liked about Ms. Simms, she didn't mince her words. She used long ones, what's more sometimes, words I didn't even know, at least I hadn't come across them in H. G. Wells or Heinlein or Asimov. She treated me like an equal, in other words — well, some of the time she treated me like an equal. For which reason I was prepared to forgive her for forgetting I didn't like football. Sometimes I'd even found myself wishing she was my aunt instead of Aunt Maggie, who treated me like I might bite if she wasn't very careful. And it's true, I might. Whereas if I bit Ms. Simms, I knew for sure she'd bite me back — like Becky, in one way. (That thought made me feel a mite happier about Becky.)

"What about my things, then?" I said. "They're at

the Milsoms? I suppose I might take them up with me now, now I've decided to stay a bit longer."

"Of course, Will. I thought it was your things you'd come for."

And to see you of course, I thought, Ms. Crafty. Ms. Check Out Will, Suss What He's Up To.

I stayed with the Milsoms that night; they asked me. They seemed properly pleased to see me. Mr. Milsom still felt like the nearest thing I had to a dad, even if he was English. But if I thought longingly of staying before I went to sleep, I didn't think so longingly of it after. I didn't hear no voices exactly. It — he — didn't hunt me that far; seemingly he didn't think he needed to. All the same he gave me nightmares. I mean it must have been him what gave me nightmares. I had them all night, the worst ones ever, like I was shut in a rock tunnel and couldn't get out, didn't no one hear me yelling. Because it was *me* yelling this time. Not no one other.

I had a Walkman in London. It was my mother's, as a matter of fact, which was why I didn't like to use it. I gave it to Becky when I arrived back at her house. I still didn't want to use it. Besides, it made up to my cousin for the one I'd gone and broken.

"I thought you said all your worldly goods were in that red squashy bag," she accused me.

"Well, they was, in a manner of speaking. This lot is my extraworldly goods," I said, making the best of it, because I still didn't really want to be here in Derbyshire, if I was honest. But it wasn't no use my going back to London. Not after the nightmares I'd been having, not after those explosive light bulbs. Whereas tonight, back at Becky's, cuddled up to Soldier, I shut my light off with no problems, slept sweet as a baby the whole night from start to finish, and didn't hear no single note of weeping.

# 7

## BECKY

I have to say I kept changing my mind about wanting Will to stay. When he said he was going back to London I was almost sorry in a way — until he threw my Walkman at the apple tree and broke it. Then all I wanted was for him to go. Next morning the light bulb exploding was the last straw. I thought it might be the same for him too. There's something funny going on with him, I don't know what it is, I only know I don't like it, and that the only way to stop it would be for him to go. So I was thrown completely when he said he was going to stay here after all.

Funnily enough though, as soon as he went down to London to see Ms. Simms and fetch his things, I missed him like anything. I got into this stupid panic that he'd still change his mind and not come back. What makes me so awkward, even to myself, let alone anyone else? Why can't I make up my mind about anything, ever? I confuse Will too, but I bet he doesn't know I confuse myself as badly. How could he guess — how could I guess, come to that — that I was actually showing I was pleased to see him by accusing him of lying the moment he got off the train, humping a great suitcase this time instead of a little squashy bag.

But he grinned, he didn't seem to hold it against me. He even let me stay in his room with him this time while he was unpacking — anybody might have thought he was pleased to see me.

Unfortunately his worldly goods weren't interesting in the least; they consisted of clothes mostly, and science fiction books. Oh, and a Walkman just like mine.

"Mum gave it to me," he said when he saw me looking at it. "I let 'er borrow it mostly. You can borrow it if you like, seeing as 'ow I broke yours."

I didn't fancy the idea much though, first off, imagining those headphones on her once-live dead ears. Maybe that was why Will hadn't brought the Walkman up last time. When I shook my head and said my Walkman would be mended any day, he put the whole thing, headphones and all, in a drawer under some sweaters. The way he closed it, you'd think he proposed never to open that drawer again in his whole life.

One other thing he had was a photograph of his mother in a broken wooden frame. He tried to hide that, too, at first, and I tried to pretend I hadn't seen it. But then he stared at me and dumped it by his bed. I didn't say anything. I even pretended not to look. But of course the moment his back was turned I did look straight at it.

It was obvious now why he hadn't recognized his mother as the fat girl in the torn-up photo. Even from where I was sitting at the end of Will's bed, I could see how thin she was. She looked about sixteen, also. I mean she had a little plait and a long skirt and a T-shirt and not much in the way of tits. (If she was that fat when she was a teenager and that thin when she was grown-up, then there was still hope for me, I thought.)

"You never told me your mum wore glasses, Will." I didn't mean to say it, it just slipped out.

"I never told you nothing about my mum," Will said, coolly.

"Only because I never asked."

"You did. And I'm still not saying. What's she got to do with you?"

Last time I'd mentioned his mother, he'd kicked me and run away. So I suppose it meant some kind of advance that this time he simply turned his back and went on putting T-shirts and things in another drawer.

Apart from that and one or two other subjects that still interested and puzzled me — some of the funny questions he'd asked me about little brothers and things, for instance — things seemed settled now, just about. Next day Mum took us both to buy school clothes, as if to prove it.

They were clothes for Will mostly; mine were new only last year and I could still get into most of them.

Actually it was fun shopping with him, much more fun than buying school clothes is usually. It felt almost like having a brother at long last. Watching Will waltz around in the shop in the vile green blazer you have to wear for the vile public school, making funny faces at me, I even thought I wouldn't mind if he were my real brother. I thought it still more when him and me started ganging up on Mum; that seemed rather mean when I thought about it later, but I have to admit it was fun at the time.

At least it was fun, till we got to Dolcis to buy shoes for both of us. For there, to my horror, sitting in the middle of the shop, one foot up on a little stool trying on the kind of lovely high-heeled court shoes that I knew my mother would never let me wear to school, was Jill Jennings, the most horrible of all the horrible girls in my class, apart from her best friend, Tracy Kent.

I pulled Mum back and said why didn't we go to Peter Lord instead, but Mum said, "What for?" and kept marching straight on in. And then it was too late anyway: Jill Jennings had seen us, her ratty little eyes (actually she's got rather big brown eyes and lots of brown curly hair and a figure like a boy's, but never mind, they are still ratty little eyes, and what's more her nose is pointed, and what's more she has thick ankles, and what's more she has thick lips) stared at us and kept on staring.

Who's he? she seemed to be asking, staring at Will.

And I suddenly saw him through her eyes — the way I'd seen him the first time I'd clapped eyes on him — and realized that any minute now I was going to have to introduce this black-eyed little titch as my cousin; as if I didn't have enough problems in that school without adding Will to them, Jill Jennings being one of the problems. Fortunately she was with her mother too that day, so she couldn't say anything. But she could look. And she did. And she could smile. Nastily. And she did.

"Was that one of your school friends?" my mother asked when we left the shop. *Friend?* I thought. Couldn't she see that the way Jill Jennings crooked up her eyebrow and twisted her mouth when she was supposedly smiling at me meant she wasn't any friend of mine? In fact, she was one of the reasons I had no friends. It was her that called me Malory Towers, after the school in the Enid Blyton books, and after that everyone called me Malory, everyone laughed at me. And all because I'd been stupid enough to admit that I had been supposed to go to boarding school, really.

"No," I said. "She's one of my school enemies."

My mother didn't answer that. I'd made no bones from the beginning about hating that school I went to. Even she seemed to realize by now that it was no good saying anything, let alone calling me silly when I made rude comments about it.

Will said, "Psst, lady, wanna hire a hit man?"

"What are your fees?" I asked, giggling.

"High," he said. "I'm the best. Hadn't you noticed?"

Not yet knowing any better, I wouldn't have bet one penny on him at that point in any contest with Jill Jennings. "I pay by results," I said firmly.

"If that's the way you want it, lady. That puts them up even higher."

He seemed very cheerful, I thought. In fact he'd been quite cheerful ever since he got back from London, give or take a bit of sharpness round questions concerning his mother. Whatever was haunting him seemed to have stopped haunting him for the moment.

The other thing was that Dad suddenly started to take notice of Will. He never took any notice of him before. He may have accepted that, blood being thicker than water, Will had to come to us; at the same time he'd made it clear from the beginning it was nothing to do with him, that he hated the whole messy business. "That tart," he'd called Megan the first evening — how long ago it seemed — adding, "What's dead's better left buried." But so he would. Dad always stays clear of anything messy or awkward; he hates getting his hands dirty, my mother says.

I know just what she means. For instance, Dad wears gloves to do the cleanest jobs in the garden, such as mowing the grass and cutting back creepers. My mother, on the other hand, hardly wears gloves at all, even in winter, except for pulling out things like nettles and brambles. She loves the feel of earth on her hands, she says. She has dirt under her nails more often than not, and the lines on her palm are sketched out in earth like lines on a map. Dad doesn't care for the feel of earth, obviously. Come to think of it, he doesn't care for gardening much at all. His fingernails and the palms of his hands are always clean as our doctor's, and cleaner.

Maybe then from my father's point of view, the business of Will seemed less messy the moment he decided to stay. Will had a green school blazer like mine, didn't he, and new school shoes. Moreover, he still hadn't shown any signs of being a window smasher or a drug taker or a shouter of four-letter words over breakfast, or a football hooligan. Judging by the cautious way Dad approached him in the beginning, Will could have been any of those things. Of course, there was the small matter of the exploding light bulbs, but you'd have to be mad to think that had anything to do with Will. (Maybe I am a bit mad, then. Maybe my mother is too; I saw the funny way she looked at Will.)

"Well, things are sorting themselves out a bit," Dad said to my mother the night Will was away. At dinner the next night, clearing his throat, he asked Will if he was interested in football.

"Not much," Will said, looking startled. Dad had

hardly addressed one word to him before. Not that Dad bothered to listen to him now. He just went on, "Well, I've a friend on the board of Derby County. Any match you want, Will, he can get us tickets. I'll see to it. Just name any match you like."

This was bad enough. But what came next was worse.

Dad said, "You'll be choosing your subjects for exams any day now then, won't you, Will? Of course, it depends what career you're thinking of. Have you given it any thought?"

I could hardly believe my ears. Dad had never asked me what career I was thinking of. Even though I wasn't thinking yet — I'd only wanted to be a vet once, for about two months, because Janey, my best friend at my old school, said she wanted to be a vet — I still didn't see why he should ask Will and not me about it, and I said so. Fortunately Will hadn't a clue what he wanted to do either, or claimed that he hadn't. Dad muttered something about putting his mind to it, "And yours too, Rebecca," he added, looking at me, but not really as if he meant it; then he fell silent, to my relief. But after dinner he suggested we all play Trivial Pursuit, so we did, just to please him; it was the first time for a long time he'd seemed interested in anything very much.

It was my turn, I remember; I was just trying to remember what year Prince Charles was born, when the lights seemed to flicker. I looked up, and in that moment I could have sworn I saw a little white face looking in through the window, level with the road. It wasn't there when I looked back. Who could it have been so close to the ground, anyway, unless it was someone mostly buried in the ground? Or unless it was a white cat? I dare say it was a white cat.

Next day Will and I put on our green blazers and our new school shoes and set off up the hill to get the school bus.

The bus was all right. No one in my class takes it. The girl who lives up the hill from me doesn't count. But who should we see standing just by the school gates when we got out but Jill Jennings.

"Good morning, Malory," she said in the mock posh accent she always puts on for my benefit, though the fact is I never had a posh accent especially, and still less so now that I'd worked on my Derbyshire accent. "That your little brother from the elementary school then, what you're minding or something?" Though of course she could perfectly well see from his blazer that he was coming to school with me.

"Mind your own business, Jill Jennings," I said, trying to push past her. "And anyway he's my cousin."

"Your cousin?" she said, eyeing his black eyes and black hair. "He doesn't look much like your cousin. Got some foreigners in your family, have you?"

"You were calling him my brother a moment ago," I said, so angry I could have hit her almost, a fact I dare say she realized; she always was very good at winding me up. Fortunately, before she could come up with anything still nastier, we saw her best crony, Tracy Kent, mincing toward us in a skirt so short you could hardly see she had a skirt on underneath her green blazer. I doubted she'd get away with it; it might be an interesting morning, I thought, finding out if she would or not. I hoped she wouldn't get away with it. No one should be allowed to have legs as good as Tracy Kent's — it isn't fair.

In other words, what with them falling on each other as if they hadn't seen each other for a month, I should have gotten Will past Jill Jennings and Tracy Kent both without further trouble, had Will let me. But he didn't. I failed to notice at first. I was marching through the gate toward the big glass-and-concrete structure that was my school, unfortunately, any proper school in my view being a tall gray stone house with dark corridors and wooden floors, above all with a proper roof; like my old school, in fact, and like the school I should have gone to. And then, suddenly, I noticed I was on my own, that Will wasn't following me.

Why should I care? was my first thought. If he didn't want me nannying him the first day, that was his right as well as his problem. But then, as usual, the possibility of blood being thicker than water got to my conscience, so I turned round, only to find Will in what seemed like deep conversation with both Jill Jennings and Tracy Kent. Goodness knows what they could have been saying to each other. I headed back toward them, dreading to think.

To my amazement, no sooner had I panted up than Jill Jennings turned and in the most amiable voice I'd ever heard her use to me — in other words, it was nine parts friendly and one part mean, instead of the other way about — said, "Well then, Malory, where did you dig him up, your little cousin? He's a scream."

"He isn't my *little* cousin," I said, sourly, not sure in my usual perverse way if I liked this turn of events. "And anyway, my name's Becky."

"Well then, *Becky,* if he's not your little cousin, who is he?" asked Tracy Kent, her voice much as usual; in other words, snide. She could afford to be snide with legs like hers, even if her hair was mud colored. Will answered before I did. "Her big one, of course," he said. For some reason they seemed to think this was very funny too. They went off into peals of laughter, more with him than at him, though, not like the way they laughed whenever I said anything. I took Will by the arm then and dragged him away.

"You'd better be careful of those two," I said as soon as we were out of earshot. "Given a chance they'll eat you for breakfast."

"Like to bet?" said Will. "How do you know I

wouldn't poison 'em, give 'em gut ache?" He made the most terrible faces; he doubled himself up. It wasn't very funny really. I don't know why I wanted to laugh so badly.

"And then they'll come back, gut ache and all, and eat you for dinner," I added severely.

"Unless I eat them first. With chips and ketchup."

"Legs and all?" I asked.

"Particularly legs," he said, in such a way it was clear he'd noticed Tracy's. Whereupon he added, making me feel much better, "Particularly fly legs. Who does she think she is? Madonna?"

I liked "fly legs." Tracy's legs were rather spindly, when I came to think of it. I felt, briefly, much better about my own.

Will was in my class, as it turned out. I didn't know whether I was glad or sorry. He didn't sit beside me, though, but at the back of the class. I was almost miffed about that, I don't know why. Tracy Kent's desk was near the back too. No one had said anything about her skirt yet, or rather, her lack of it.

My desk was between Susan Baker's and Zakky Thompson's. I didn't mind either of them, even though Zakky's name was really Zachariah, and coming from a family of religious freaks, he'd hand you a load about Jesus given half a chance. He'd never offered me a nasty word, on the other hand, nor did he seem to give a toss that I never felt like discussing Jesus, his forgiveness of sins and all that. My sins, I knew, Zakky had told me, bled as freely as he described Jesus' heart doing for all of us, but that didn't mean I wanted to talk about them to him. Usually, before he could get going properly, I'd start to talk about homework instead, or "Top of the Pops." "Top of the Pops" always seemed to interest Zakky a lot. (This was surprising, given that they didn't have a television at his house. He wasn't allowed to listen to pop music on the radio either. He only ever heard it in the shops or at school on someone else's Walkman.)

Our new class teacher this year was Mr. Peters. I knew him a bit. He was the history teacher who'd started teaching us about the industrial revolution in the summer term. This term, he told us — we had history straight after break — he was going to continue that, but with particular reference to the industrial history of these parts: mines, cotton mills, and so forth.

If he sounded enthusiastic at the prospect, it was more than could be said for the class. Someone — Dean Onslow, of course — groaned, very loudly. Mr. Peters fell silent hearing that. His gaze swept the room; gradually it got nearer to where Dean Onslow was sitting, swinging neatly back and forth past him, like the pendulum on the grandfather clock in the hall of our house; getting slower and slower, like the same pendulum when my father forgot to wind the clock, finally stopping altogether — on Dean Onslow, of course. For a moment Mr. Peters looked at him, still silent. But then he shouted; just two words was enough. "Get lost." Dean Onslow looked as if he wished he could get lost.

(He's like that, Mr. Peters. You'd think he was asleep half the time, he seems so tired and bored. And then suddenly he'll strike, like a snake curled up asleep one moment, striking dead on target the next. He even wore snake colors usually: goldy-browny-greeny tweed jackets. Gold or brown or green ties.)

There was more silence afterward. Such silence you could have heard a pin drop. Of course, no one actually had a pin to drop, but after a minute or so I did hear a rustle behind me that I wouldn't have picked up normally: the sound of someone's arm going up.

"Yes?" said Mr. Peters, staring beyond me. He was looking sleepy again, his right set of fingers soundlessly tapping at his desk.

"Sir," said a familiar voice, in the London accent that was so familiar by now I was really getting quite fond of it, I realized. "Sir. I got a question. About them mines and miners. Did miners used to get lost down them sometimes? Are there ghosts ever of miners round here, what got stuck down mines? Was there any ever?"

You could have knocked me down with a feather. What did he have to go and ask that for? I wondered,

105

hearing the titters round me. Seeing Mr. Peters's not-quite-smiling face.

"Anyone would think — what's your name then, boy — aren't you new?" He didn't wait for an answer. "Anyone would think I taught English literature — fiction — but I don't, I'm a historian, my lad, it's fact, it's the truth I'm after."

Even the sarcasm in his voice couldn't seem to stop Will now. "It mightn't be true," he insisted, "that there was a ghost. But people thinking there was, thinking they heard things, might be true."

"True or not, it ain't history," said Mr. Peters. "Not in my book. It's more psychology on the one hand, folklore on the other. There's plenty of stuff on local folklore, if that's what you're after, Will." (I was interested that he'd remembered Will's name this time round, after less than an hour or so in his company. But it was true, Mr. Peters always could remember names when it was important, as, evidently, he thought this discussion was. All the rest of the time he called you "er" or "um," if not "girl" or "boy.") "I don't have to repeat it, do I? I teach history, not fiction. On the other hand there are plenty of monographs — that's pamphlets to you — on local folklore. I'll bring some in for you, if you like. And maybe we can discuss in this class why folklore isn't history. Another time," he added hastily, "another time." Why he sounded in such a hurry about it, I don't know, because no one seemed interested in starting up a discussion. I wasn't interested. All I was thinking about still was Will.

For instance, I was thinking about those times he'd seemed so scared about so little, the time he heard the child crying in the cave, the time I got stuck in the mine shaft. Did he know something I didn't? And if so, why didn't he ask me? He didn't need Mr. Peters's pamphlets. Everyone round us knew about the boy who got lost in a mine shaft and was said to be heard crying sometimes. Not that anyone I knew had ever heard him; they only knew someone else who had.

This terrible thought now came to me. Will hadn't heard him, had he? It couldn't be more than a story, could it? There couldn't really be a ghost. And if there was a ghost, what did it have to do with Will, why should he hear it, why not me? Not that I wanted to hear it. The very idea frightened me to death.

# 8

## W I L L

So Mr. Peters thinks only history is true, does he, not stories? Speaking as someone who always used to want them to be true, science fiction stories in particular, at this moment in my life I wanted him to be right. I wanted people to stay in their own time and space and not bother no one outside them. That's what I wanted.

Mr. Peters did bring me some of his booklets, though. There was a boy, I found out. Nearly two hundred years ago it had been, when boys like me got sent down mines, I mean the really narrow ones no one else could go in. In one cave we went to they'd told us how the boys wore hats with lamps and the lamps was fueled by carbon monoxide, which is poisonous. If the lamp went out for lack of air the kids would be in trouble. They used to make the mothers sit at the top, pumping the air in; the mothers wouldn't want their little kids to die, of course, of carbon monoxide poisoning or of nothing else; well, you'd assume so. You'd assume they'd keep on pumping. But me, I could believe most things of most mothers, remembering how mine was, how she'd invited in that Mike, and what he did to me, how she killed herself in the end, leaving me alone in the world. Blood is thicker than water, Aunt Maggie keeps saying. Is it? I wonder.

Because this mother, you see, didn't pump hard enough; that's how the story goes. Even if it wasn't history I could believe it, no problem. This kid's lamp went out, sometime. He was deep down too, a bit deeper than no one wanted to go in to find him, so they left him there. Left him to rot. You'd have thought they'd have gotten him out at least and given him a decent burial.

No one in the booklet seems quite sure where all this happened, either. People had heard crying in most of the mines, they said. There wasn't no one who actually had heard it, only lots of people knew someone had heard it.

Well, I've got news for them. I'd heard it. I mean the crying. And I knew which mine it was, most likely. The one with the shaft near us, which Becky and me had passed that morning.

"But it's all filled in. You couldn't get in there to have a look if you wanted," Becky said, when we was talking about it.

In fact it was her started us talking about it. She marched into my room one evening when I was doing my homework and asked me straight out if I'd heard this ghost ever, or something like it. Not quite looking at me one moment, then staring me straight in the eye, daring me to say yes — or no, it wasn't clear which she wanted.

I was sitting at the table Aunt Maggie had put up there for me near the window, my feet on Soldier. He'd taken to keeping me company during the evening while I was doing my homework, as well as through the nights.

"When you asked me if I had a little brother that first morning, that was it, wasn't it?" she insisted, and added, glowering at Soldier, "What's he doing here? You know he's not allowed upstairs in the bedrooms."

I didn't answer that question. I told her about the crying I kept hearing. The voice that said "Help me." It was a relief, in a way, much more than I expected. I'd been alone in too many things in my life not to be glad I wasn't alone in this one no longer.

"Why didn't you tell me before then?" she complained. "Did you want me to think you'd gone barmy? I did think you'd gone barmy. Maybe you are barmy. Maybe it's just voices in your head. Isn't that supposed to be one of the first signs of madness?"

I thought about that. The crying had been a bit different lately. It did sound more as if it was coming from inside my head. Also it seemed to be there when I was asleep as well as when I was awake, grumbling away behind my dreams, like it was biding its time for

110

the moment, waiting. I can't say I liked it. One or two nights I'd woken up crying with it. On the other hand, it didn't sound so desperate as it had done. Merely by staying I seemed to have done what it wanted. As well as what I wanted, I realized suddenly and then wished I hadn't realized.

I'd felt sad rather than angry lately. At the same time calm, holding myself in, not stirring myself up, not wanting to stir no one else up for that matter. It wasn't my fault I stirred Becky up merely by existing. She certainly seemed stirred up at the moment. She was the one who seemed angry at the moment.

Take school, for instance. School was all right, at least I thought so. Much better than some I'd been to. Becky, though, said she hated it. She'd hardly no friends to speak of, and it wasn't the others' fault entirely. I mean the way she stood looking at everyone, angrily, suspiciously, as if waiting for them to say something nasty so she could get upset. Naturally they said nasty things, who wouldn't? And then she got upset. And said nasty things in her turn, the way she had to me when I first came to Derbyshire.

She reminded me of someone. After a bit I realized it was my mother. Mum used to behave in exactly the same way sometimes. Becky even looked like my mother sometimes, I noticed, horrified. Why hadn't I noticed it before? I wondered. She wasn't bad looking, only a bit plumpish. And getting a bit thinner, it seemed to me, these days.

Tracy and Jill didn't do me no harm, anyway; they called me Titch and asked me to sit with them at school lunches; not that I ever did, if I could help it, especially after they told me they liked my black hair and started asking questions about my mum and dad. I kept them off Becky's back, though, or tried to, not that she was grateful. If anything, it made her angrier than ever. Like me turning out to be good at math and things made her angry. Like me becoming good friends with Zakky Thompson made her angry.

For Zakky and me was good friends by then, even in spite of his having tried out his Jesus bit on me. When I told him straight off I wasn't interested in Jesus, his bright yet deep-set blue eyes gazed at me so hard, so directly, I couldn't hardly take in what the rest of his face was saying. But I swear one little corner of his mouth moved. One little corner of his mouth smiled against the habit of the rest of his face, which didn't.

"Right," he agreed amiably. "Right, no Jesus. Except on Sundays."

"But there ain't no school on Sundays," I objected.

"Of course there isn't," said Zakky. "Don't you see, that's the point." Well, I didn't see really. But I didn't care, provided Zakky kept his promise. And he did, apart from intoning words like "Praise be the Lord" every now and then. I could never be sure if he wanted

me to take them seriously, in spite of everything. Or
if he just liked the sound. Or if he was just doing it to
tease me.

It could have been any of those things. Zakky was
like that, I'd begun to realize. Maybe that was why no
one teased him, never mind all his Jesus talk in a voice
surprisingly deep considering it hadn't yet broken, never
mind the weird way he looked with his sticking-up ears
and sticking-up hair. He was very tall, too, as well as
thin. With my being so short he and I must have looked
strange, going around together. Goodness knows why
I found him so comforting to be with. I couldn't even
make him laugh, or rarely.

I couldn't make Becky laugh now, either. Not that
she let on. When she saw other people laughing at
me — even when making them laugh was how I'd
stopped them laughing at her — she just got angrier
than ever.

The thing what made her angriest of all, though,
wasn't nothing to do with school. It was the way her
dad seemed to have taken to me suddenly. You should
have seen her glaring at us when he talked to me about
football — he still didn't cotton on I wasn't interested
in football, no matter how many times I told him. He
kept promising to take me to watch Derby County.
He'd say, "They're playing Forest next Saturday (or
Spurs, or Sheffield Wednesday). How about it, Will?"
Aunt Maggie would offer to get tickets for us, even. But

Uncle Jim always said, "No, no, I'll ring my friend on the Board." But he never did, thank goodness.

A few times Becky said, on my behalf, "But Will doesn't like football." But neither of them heard her. And after a bit she seemed to fancy the idea I'd have to go and spend the afternoon doing something I hated, so she said nothing. She just got angry, that's all, angrier and angrier. It was like she took all my anger, it was like the boy was yelling in her head now instead of mine.

I even asked her one day if she'd managed to hear my ghost yet.

"No," she said angrily, "no, I haven't. Anyway," she added, "who says it's your ghost? It's ours. You heard it in our house, didn't you? You're hearing it in our house, aren't you? Are you still hearing it? Is it still saying 'Help me'? What are you doing about it? How can you help it?"

And I still didn't know, neither. On Saturday afternoons sometimes I went to the mound where the shaft used to be. I don't know why they'd bothered to put a fence round it. You'd never know there had been a hole there even. Once, on a dry afternoon just before half term, the leaves in the wood below it red and brown and yellow, alongside red berries I didn't know the name of, I climbed over the fence and lay down beside the gray stone and put my ear to the green grass and listened with all my might.

"Are you there?" I whispered. "Can you hear

me? You don't need to cry, I'm here, just tell me."

But I didn't hear nothing. Not a whisper, except from birds and sheep and wind and dry leaves, the usual kinds of things you hear in the country, that I was beginning to get quite used to — that I was beginning to get quite fond of. I don't know if I was glad or not. I was certainly maddened. Why should he plague me in my own room, I thought, and not here where he should be? Would I hear him if I came at night? I was not bloody going to come here in the night, though, not bloody likely.

Next weekend I asked Zakky Thompson over and took him to see the shaft. His parents wouldn't have let him come if he'd told them where he was going. I don't know what he'd pretended instead, but he came, anyway, and my aunt seemed to think it was all quite in order. She even seemed pleased I'd invited a friend over.

"Why don't you have a friend for tea too?" she asked Becky, not seeming to have the faintest idea that this was a silly question. She and Becky didn't understand nothing about each other these days, I'd noticed.

I told Becky she could come with Zakky and me if she wanted, but she just shook her head sourly. Not that I cared much. I was so fed up with her these days, I really preferred just to be with Zakky. Not least Zakky didn't ever, one little bit, look like my mother.

Like I said, Zakky didn't look like no one. He was a real alien. Maybe we both was. Maybe the day was soon coming when we'd reveal it to each other and then to all the earthlings. In a way we had already revealed it to each other. I told him about the ghost, for instance, and he didn't turn a hair. He just believed me.

"Maybe," he said, "you're his reincarnation." Though reincarnation was something we'd discussed a few times — it shows how different Zakky was that he wanted to discuss such matters — this wasn't a thought I cared for. So I didn't believe him. If I'm honest I didn't dare believe him.

It was quite a damp day, if not actually raining. This did not stop Zakky. He lay flat on the ground where the shaft used to be and put his ear to it. "It sounds hollow," he said. But that was all he said he heard; he couldn't hear no crying.

When he got up again he was covered in grass and mud. "What's your mum going to say?" I asked him. He looked at me with his blue-chip eyes steady. He said, "I'll say I got carried away praying."

He might have meant it, too — I could imagine Zakky carried away praying. He got carried away in class sometimes and discussed history or English as if he was preaching. He did preach in his church, he said, when he was asked to. He got carried away now, but not with talking. He started heaving away at the stones where the shaft should have been. He managed to shift one a little bit. I helped him, but then neither of us quite dared, after all, to go no further. Not even Zakky, the ultimate alien, dared go no further. Maybe he was hungry — it was already past teatime.

I needn't have worried about the grass and mud he'd gathered. Aunt Maggie cleaned Zakky up beautifully, sponged his jeans over, and hung them to dry on the stove. He insisted on covering his scraggy flanks with a towel though, before sitting down to tea in his underpants and letting her feed him rock cakes from one of her bring-and-buy sales, plus chocolate chip cookies and banana sandwiches. That was another thing about Zakky — thin as he was, he always ate like there wouldn't be no nosh tomorrow. Aunt Maggie looked at him after a bit and offered him beefburgers. He ate those too, with oven chips and ketchup. It wasn't as if he'd get no supper at home, later. He would, I know; I asked him.

Becky guessed where Zakky and I'd been all afternoon. "You've told Zakky Thompson about it. I mean the ghost," she accused me, next morning.

"Why shouldn't I tell Zakky?" I asked airily.

Becky shrugged. Her eyes filled with tears. "As if you don't know," she answered.

Becky mournful was still worse than Becky angry. What with her being mournful one minute and angry the next I wished it wasn't half term. I could have done with Tracy Kent and Jill Jennings giggling and bitching, I could have done with Mr. Peters in his snake-colored clothes and snaky bite going on about Richard Arkwright and the stupidity of all of us. Above all I could have done with Zakky. But he had to stay at home the rest of the week, he'd said when I asked him. The only company, not to say comfort, around was Soldier. It rained every day, just about, to make things worse. Even the rooks in the wood across the road sounded sorry for themselves.

Was the ghost getting wet too? I wondered. At least was its bones getting wet, in the deep tunnel where they was lying? For surely there was bones down in a tunnel somewhere; and surely, as with all caves and tunnels I'd been into, the rain leaked down into it little by little. Perhaps that's why its voice suddenly started sounding more desperate again, waking me up, making my heart turn over. Or perhaps it was just the date, the time of year: the thirty-first of October, almost.

"Halloween. All Souls' Day," said Aunt Maggie. "Time for witches."

On the day of Halloween itself she stood at the kitchen table hollowing out a huge turnip to make a lantern. "In America children go off tricking and treating," she told us.

"That's just for babies," Becky said sourly.

As for me, I hadn't never heard of no such thing and told them I hadn't.

"Your mother and I didn't go tricking and treating,"

said Aunt Maggie, putting the insides of the turnip in a saucepan for soup. (She'd rather taken to saying "Your mother and I" lately. I wished she wouldn't.) "Your mother and I hadn't heard of it either. No one did it up here, in those days, when we were your age. We used to make turnip lanterns, though. We used to duck for apples. That was fun, ducks."

There and then she insisted on filling a red plastic washing-up bowl with water and throwing in some big green Granny Smith apples; she set the whole thing down on the quarry-tiled floor and made Becky and me duck for apples, just as she had. But fun it wasn't. No one couldn't get their teeth around apples big as those ones. All it did was make us wet, and wetter, and angrier with each other. For two pins I'd've upped and tipped that bowl and all its contents over Becky. For two pins, by the look of her, she'd have tipped the bowl over me.

During supper that night — Uncle Jim was out for some reason — the turnip lantern flickered on the sideboard in the dining room, throwing mean shadows. There was a huge bowl of fruit beside it, oranges, apples, bananas, grapes, and plums and peaches. All round the turnip Aunt Maggie had stacked tomatoes and little gourds and trails of little red leaves and seed pods. It was meant to look pretty, I suppose, and it did look quite pretty — it was just the sort of thing my mother would have made, I thought, wanting, instantly, to pull the whole lot to pieces.

Tossing food around on the plate with her fork, Becky said scornfully, "It looks like harvest festival, not like Halloween. Do you suppose there are witches outside?" she added, staring at the window. "We don't need any witches. I'll be the witch and frighten off all the souls." Now she was looking at me. "I'd like to make sure they don't bother us any longer."

"Have some more risotto," said Aunt Maggie, offering me a full spoonful. But I wasn't Zakky Thompson. I couldn't go on eating forever. Besides, I was thinking of all those lost souls out there, up in the sky or under the earth. I didn't know which I thought was worse, to be among the stars or down in the fiery wheels of the earth, among the dinosaurs and that. I used to know. I think I used to know. But I didn't know nothing no longer. I found myself wishing I was Zakky Thompson, knowing how to preach Jesus. It wouldn't matter if I didn't believe it to start with. All I needed was to know how to preach him, I thought, and then I would believe it.

Becky didn't want no risotto neither. She seemed to have lost her big appetite lately. She took an orange from the fruit bowl on the sideboard and like an afterthought blew out the candle in the turnip lantern. In the smell of smoke and burning, she peeled the orange with a knife and ate it, section by section, her face grinning angrily like the face on the hollow turnip.

"Help me," the voice said all night, in dream and waking. "Help me." In one of my dreams it added, "I can't breathe. My lamp's gone out." But I was too busy crying for my own lost mother to take notice; even though I knew that crying for my own lost mother made me know what he felt. "If you can hear him, why can't I?" Becky kept on asking me, and that was why: *her* mother hadn't pushed her down a mine, her mother hadn't abandoned her, so how could she understand him? But I could. It's not just that blood is thicker than water, as Aunt Maggie keeps on saying; understanding someone else's feelings is thicker than water too. And no one understood mine except that ghost, and no one understood his except me — that was what I felt. And I knew that though I was ignoring his cries now, the day was shortly coming when I wouldn't be able to anymore; that I'd not be allowed to resist a dead soul's cries much longer. And that even now, any minute there'd be trouble for it; there must be.

Sure enough, in the morning, when I came down to breakfast, I heard these strange sounds of bounding and swishing. I found fruit in the air, up and down, bouncing and flying.

# 9

## BECKY

It was the strangest sight, all those oranges and apples and zucchini and things dancing in the air. Only the turnip lantern still sat in its same place, unmoving, grinning at everything else. I wondered about lighting it; I don't know why I did — I mean what would have been the point? It might even have encouraged the lantern to start hopping about with the rest of the stuff; we might get a fire on top of everything. Perhaps, the way I'd been feeling lately, that's what I really wanted.

But of course I didn't light it. To have reached the turnip I would have had to move away from the safe place in which I was standing, and much as I was enjoying the weird sight it made no sense to get in the way of the fruits and vegetables bouncing up and down, dancing. An orange might be nice to eat, I thought, but it mightn't seem so nice hitting you on the nose or giving you a black eye. I'd no doubt an orange could give you a black eye if it came at you hard enough. It's as solid as a rubber ball at least, probably solider.

I wasn't frightened at first. I don't know why. Such unlikely happenings ought to have frightened me. When I think about it now, I can even make myself start shaking. At the time, though, I found myself laughing out loud, feeling better than I had for ages. I might have engineered the whole thing myself, the bouncing and swishing sounds — and one squelch as a tomato hit the ground a bit too hard for its own good and rose rather heavily and awkwardly, dripping a few seeds and juices — might have been all my own achievement. In fact between me and that angry ghost, I still can't be sure it wasn't.

I only got frightened when I heard Will enter the room behind me. For then, all at once the fruits and vegetables — golden oranges, green apples, red tomatoes, the two clumsy bunches of grapes swaying fatly like udders, rather bruised-looking plums and peaches, zucchini like thick green arrows, bananas like yellow boomerangs — stopped dancing in their places, pointed viciously in our direction, started moving, bouncing, darting, rotating, toward us. Someone invisible might have been throwing them at us — or at Will, anyway. I certainly had the feeling that it was my bad luck I happened to be in the way, that I wasn't the real target of this angry greengrocery's onslaught.

Will was still near the door, fortunately. He got out and slammed it, not a very gentlemanly act, seeing how he left me on the other side, alone and unprotected.

Luckily for him — and me — not much hit me. I felt little swishings of air as the fruits went past: A banana grazed my cheek, a tomato slid by my head, an orange nestled in the crook of my arm for a moment, then fell heavily to the floor. All the rest of the attackers, the apples, oranges, grapes, plums, tomatoes, and so forth, thudded against the door and fell back weakly. Some things, the tomatoes, for instance, and the grapes, left quite a lot of themselves on the door. Its nice white panels were soon a mess of grape skins, tomato seeds, and so forth. Most of the stuff that landed on the floor, in fact, looked so much the worse for wear, it was hard to imagine how prettily my mother had arranged them, how delightful the fruits and vegetables had looked dancing in the air together.

I didn't even know that my mother had entered the room until suddenly I heard her shouting at me. That is, I assumed she was shouting at me, although it wasn't my name that came out of her mouth at that moment. "Megan!" she shouted. And again, "Megan!" For a second I almost believed that she was right to call me that, that I actually was her sister, Megan, at that moment.

As I came to my senses, though, so did she. Very stiffly and calmly, she dumped two plates of scrambled eggs down on the table, and asked, "What do you think you're doing, Rebecca? Have you quite taken leave of your senses?"

"What do you mean, what am I doing? I'm not doing anything," I protested. It was reasonable, I suppose, to be indignant at the time, but now I can see all too well that the conclusions she jumped to were even more reasonable, considering.

"Do you expect me to believe that the fruit was throwing itself?" she replied, angrily. "Duck, I wasn't born yesterday. Those eggs'll be cold before you're ready to eat them," she added, "but that's not my fault, is it? You're going to clear this whole lot up, first. Every single bit of it, Rebecca."

Her voice trailed away. She sat down at the table in my place, not her own, cleared a plate and placemat out of the way carefully, then, to my hórror, put her head down on her hands as if she were about to burst into tears.

But she did not burst into tears, not yet, anyway. Instead she looked up at me perfectly dry-eyed. "Do you do it on purpose, Becky? Being so like Megan?"

My mother recovered herself pretty quickly, I must say. She was even kind enough to put our scrambled eggs back in the oven after all. Though they were hard by the time we got to eat them — not that I was very hungry — at least they weren't cold. Afterward Will looked at me sideways and went out. His slamming of the door behind him might have been accidental, but I doubt it.

Seeing the bruised fruit back in the fruit bowl next to the turnip lantern, as I cleared away the dishes, seeing the zucchini heaped up in the vegetable rack in the kitchen, I felt frightened for the first time. After a bit I turned the grinning face of the turnip to the wall. Even that wasn't enough to reassure me. Eventually, when my mother wasn't looking, I took it out to the kitchen and dumped it in the big wastebin on top of all the ruined vegetables and fruit. Yet that still did not stop me from seeing the bouncing oranges, the cavorting tomatoes, the spinning green apples, the swaying clusters of grapes with their little empty green spits from which the fruit had been pulled and eaten in the way my mother always complained of.

"Why don't you cut one whole bunch off at a time," I could hear her saying. At that, suddenly, it was me who wanted to burst into tears of shock and disbelief. And so I did, sitting at the kitchen table. I felt I didn't understand anything at the moment, least of all myself, the way I'd been behaving, the anger I was feeling.

"Why are you so perverse, Becky?" was my mother's most frequent question. Why are *you* so perverse? I wondered, because it did seem perverse to me the way she had changed since we first heard about Megan. If she was grieving, how could she grieve about someone lost longer than I'd been alive for? Had she loved Megan more than she loved me? I hated her for it, almost. At the same time I wanted everything to be as before. I wanted her to cuddle me like a baby and stroke me and say it didn't matter. This didn't stop me, when she laid a hand on my shoulder, from pushing it off at once, perverse as usual, cutting off my own nose to spite my own face, as much and more than anyone else's.

"What do you mean about Megan? About me being like her?" I demanded. And of course I really wanted to know, but I also wanted to upset my mother, to punish her, for assuming it had been me throwing fruit and so forth, for her likely refusal to believe me when I denied it. At the same moment I wanted to fling my arms round her neck and beg her to forgive me. Why *are* you so perverse, Becky? I wondered.

Mum didn't say anything at first. She opened one of the stove lids and started scrubbing the hot plate with the special wire brush. At last she flung at me over her shoulder, "I meant you are like Megan. A little bit."

"I'm fat," I said.

"Don't be stupid, Becky. I don't mean that."

"I *am* stupid. Was Megan stupid?"

"Becky, I just meant you looked like Megan. It's not surprising. She was my twin sister. Will looks a bit like her too. She was his mother."

"Have you been looking at me all these years and thinking I looked like someone you weren't ever going to tell me existed?" I inquired.

"Becky!" she said.

"You're always saying 'Becky!' these days," I said.

"If you're not saying 'Megan!' Why did you say 'Megan' when that fruit . . ." I hesitated — I didn't quite know how I was going to put this. I didn't want to make it sound as if I actually had been throwing the stuff — I hadn't been throwing it, had I? — I was so confused I could almost believe anything at the moment. I could feel the tears beginning to course down my cheeks again already. "When the fruit was sort of flying?"

My mother finished one side of the stove, slammed the lid down, picked up the other, and scrubbed that hot plate too. I don't know what good it did. Her mind didn't seem on the job exactly. The strokes of the brush got slower and slower. Eventually she gave up altogether, set the lid back down, gently this time, and hung the brush up on its hook behind the stove. Then to my horror she came and sat down at the table next to me.

She didn't try to touch me this time, though. She sat and looked at me for a minute while I looked away from her and wondered why she was pussyfooting about. Why does she always have to be so moral about everything? I wondered. Why can't she just say I'm horrible and be done with it? Once upon a time she would have done. Maybe we would have both laughed afterward. Now neither of us was laughing, not even at the stupid apron she was wearing. The words PRIZE COOK were written in red across her large bosom over a picture of a pig with a laurel wreath about its white chef's hat.

"Did she go in for throwing fruit about?" I asked. "Megan, I mean. I don't throw fruit about," I said, desperately, knowing my mother wouldn't, she *couldn't* believe me, that she had to keep thinking it was me who had done it.

"Lying won't help, duck," she said mechanically. But then she went on as if, at this moment, the subject was much more interesting to her. "She did throw a whole load of fruit once, Megan. We had a terrible fight, she and I. It was at the table in the middle of lunch, there was a bowl of fruit on the table for dessert, she picked up every piece one by one, starting with the messiest and threw it at me. She broke a plate and at least three glasses. You've never seen such a mess. She had her pocket money docked for three whole months afterward."

"How much pocket money *did* you get in those days?" I asked.

She looked at me then, amazedly, as if she couldn't think what that had to do with it. Before she could say anything, however, I threw in a much more important question.

"What's it like having a twin sister?" I asked her. I was remembering suddenly how, years ago, I used to imagine I had a twin myself. How I used to lie in bed with my eyes closed tight pretending that when

I opened them I'd find lying alongside me in a bed identical to my own a real twin sister, like me in all the ways I wanted and different from me in all the ways I wanted. I'd given up those dreams long before Will arrived, of course. I'd almost forgotten them. But now it occurred to me to wonder if they hadn't been reasonable dreams to have, had I but known it.

"Don't twins usually have twins? I mean, don't twins run in families, I mean, couldn't I have been one?" I persisted, even though by then it seemed a waste of time asking her anything. For she still had not answered either of my other questions, nor showed any sign of doing so. Indeed, she'd gotten up from the table again and was standing at the stove, filling up mugs with hot water out of the kettle. Coffee, I thought as she dumped mine on the table in front of me. Since when had she let me have coffee, let alone *assumed* I'd like some? The two identical mugs — except that I put a spoonful of sugar in mine — made me feel happier suddenly. "Why am I not a twin?" I insisted, cradling my hands round my comfortable green mug.

"I'm told it usually skips a generation. You're more likely to have twins yourself, Becky, than I was. Or Megan," she added, reluctantly, as if she were making herself say it.

"What's it like having a twin?" I repeated. "That's what I really want to know. Why won't you tell me?"

130

But my mother, so usually ready to flood me with information, still seemed unwilling or unable to do so. She sighed and stirred her coffee. After a full minute it seemed like, she said, almost angrily, "How should I know, Becky, what it was like? I was never anything else, I never thought. It just seemed normal."

I pressed on. Though I knew what dangerous territory I was entering, I knew how the name Megan set my mother off. I could not help it: I really had to know. "All right then, what was it like being *Megan*'s twin? Or just even Megan's *sister?*"

My mother sighed again. "Megan?" she said. "Oh yes, Megan. Just imagine," she said, as if I had at last pressed the right key and she could talk. "Just imagine, duck, competing with someone from the very moment you were born; from before you were born. Just imagine having someone else to compare yourself with from the moment you were born. For other people to compare you with. Megan can read now. Why can't you read yet, Margaret? Margaret's got a pretty doll, have *you* got one, Megan? Megan's wearing a blue dress today, Margaret, why are you wearing a *red* one? Margaret's trying for university, Megan, why aren't *you* trying?"

"Did you mind that?" I prompted her. "Did you mind people comparing you and that sort of thing? Did you mind wearing a red dress when she was wearing a blue one?"

My mother took a swallow of her coffee and set her

cup down again. "Did I mind?" she asked. "No, I don't think so. Well, if I did mind it wasn't half as much as Megan minded. She hated it. She hated people comparing us. She wanted us to be exactly the same so people wouldn't have to compare us. That was what she said. But then she got fat, so it was obvious we were different. She always was perverse, Megan."

There it was, that word again. Perverse. "Like me," I said in a small voice. My mother actually laughed. "Yes, like you, my duck." And gave me an affectionate pat on the shoulder. "I dare say you inherited it."

"And did you like being a twin?" I asked her. "*Did* you?"

"Like it? How could I like it or not like it? As I said, I didn't know any different. The fact I wanted to strangle Megan sometimes is neither here nor there. I dare say she wanted to strangle me sometimes. In fact, I know she did."

"Were you the bossy one?" I asked, though certain of it.

"Megan always said so."

"You're still pretty bossy sometimes," I ventured.

She looked startled. "Of course I am. I'm your mother."

"You weren't Megan's mother," I pointed out.

"No, I wasn't. But she treated me just like one. I thought that after, after she went. I remembered how I used to say to her, 'Do it yourself, Megan, I'm not your mother.' I mean, she expected me to trail along behind her picking things up, sorting out all the trouble she got into. Oh, it never ended. Oh, how angry she made me."

"And then she ran away," I said.

"What's that got to do with it, Becky?"

"Nothing," I said saucily, looking at her, blaming her, thinking I knew why Megan ran away, angry with Megan at the same time for upsetting my mother so badly. I could see tears glinting in her eyes again. Mothers didn't have any business crying, I thought, it was too upsetting. She was perverse. Megan was perverse. I was perverse. Everyone in the world was perverse — why can't people be normal and ordinary and get along with each other? I wondered. Why can't I? I love my mother, don't I? My mother must have loved Megan; Megan must have loved her. What was wrong with everyone? And why did we suffer so much wrongness so many years after it all happened? Like Megan. Like Will's ghost. Though I didn't doubt any longer Will heard a ghost of some sort, I couldn't tell if it had been behind the flying fruit — maybe I had thrown the fruit in my anger, after all. Or maybe we both had. It wasn't a question I was going to think about, for the moment. I'd had enough of ghosts, for the moment. Yet there remained one small question I couldn't stop myself from asking.

"Did you used to tell Megan what to think always?"

I inquired in a small voice and immediately wished I hadn't.

My mother gave me a bewildered smile and suddenly I wasn't angry anymore, just sad. Suddenly I'd had enough of this conversation also. I just went round the table and hugged her, my lovely big and bossy mother in her blue fisherman's jersey and shiny prize apron.

School started again on Monday. On Thursday Mr. Peters was taking our class to Matlock Bath. We were going up in the cable car and down into a real mine. Then, I thought, we shall see what we shall see. Jill Jennings and Tracy Kent can do their worst, I thought, laying my head on my mother's slippery bosom, which smelled of onions and butter and stove brush, altogether delightful. How glad I was at that moment that she was my mother and not Megan; that Megan wasn't my mother and she was. Poor Will, I thought. Poor Will. Because he was Megan's son, not Margaret's. Because he hadn't got a mother anymore, had only half had his mother, ever. And it was then that I understood, perhaps for the first time, why Will could hear the ghost and I couldn't. It felt as if the crying, the little white face in the window, belonged to Will my cousin, as well as to the ghost; that the ghost's crying was Will's crying also — and that just as Will and I were bound together by blood, by cousinship, he and the ghost, lost in the earth, divided from their mothers, were bound together by pain and fear and grief. I realized that grief, too, was thicker than water, at the same time I saw that this was something I couldn't share with Will, not yet. Even my mother couldn't share it with him, entirely, for all her grief. Yes, Megan had been her twin sister, but she had been Will's mother.

# 10

## W I L L

Becky didn't seem to mind the fruit going crazy the way I did. She even seemed more cheerful afterward. I couldn't understand it. At least we hadn't seen the photograph being torn up; at least I'd only heard my ghost, never seen it. But we'd seen all that fruit flying about all right, like someone was throwing the stuff at me. That gave me the creeps straight up — never mind what it did, or didn't do, to Becky. There was some funny business going on in her house, certain. I felt most of it had to do with me, yet it couldn't all be me, entirely. For instance, one night the voice in my room said, "Bury me," as well as "Help me." It only said it just the once, but that was enough to alarm me. I mean, ghosts don't have bodies, do they, by definition?

I was glad to go back to school the following Monday morning. In the afternoon, during the last half-hour before going-home time, Mr. Peters read out the cast for the Christmas pantomime his class always does each year. It was Cinderella this term. Every one of us had been made to audition for it the week before half term. The girls had almost all chosen to audition for Cinderella, of course, even Becky, though she only tried because I told her she'd be chicken if she didn't.

It was just as well she'd listened. Though I still don't know why she listened, seeing as how she didn't usually, she got the part all right. Maybe in one way Mr. Peters was being nice to her. He might look dopey and sleepy, but he always knew what was going on around him, at least when it mattered.

But I don't think he was only being nice to Becky, or no one else for that matter. I'd been surprised how well she'd read the part. When Cinders was told she couldn't go to the ball she'd sounded properly unhappy. Then when the Prince came to find her — Dean Onslow was reading for the Prince at that point, so she could only have been acting — her eyes shone, her voice shook, she sounded so pleased it was like she really thought he had come.

She looked more pleased still when Mr. Peters read her name out. So did the people round her. Zakky Thompson, for instance, thumped her on the back. I think some of the others, though, was pleased because the part hadn't gone to Jill Jennings or Tracy Kent. As the prettiest girls in the class one of them had been expecting to get it. A few girls even sniggered and gave them a sideways look, while Susan Baker, who sat next to Becky said, "Well done, Becks" so loudly it was obvious she meant everybody else to hear. (It was only me who called Becky "Becks," as a rule.)

Tracy and Jill *wasn't* pleased, of course. Even Jill being made the Fairy Godmother didn't seem to mollify them much. It was lucky for Becky, I thought, that they hadn't been made the Ugly Sisters; two boys was playing them. Deirdre Smith, the tallest girl in the class, was to be Prince Charming.

"Whoever heard of a one-hundred-and-fifty-pound Cinderella?" said Tracy.

Jill, her voice mean and sweet together, said, "I've got a card somewhere for Weight Watchers, Malory, sorry, Becks, if you'd like it."

"No thanks," said Becky ferociously. "By the way, my name is Becky. Rebecca to you." And in fact she'd gotten so much thinner these days, she didn't need to go to Weight Watchers. Maybe her legs wasn't as good as Tracy Kent's, but so what, she didn't have to wear a tunic and tights, not like Prince Charming.

I'd read for Buttons myself, in my best London accent. Of course I got the part, it was what you'd call typecasting. Not that I felt much like playing no one at the moment. For two nights I'd hardly seemed to sleep. When I was awake the voice muttered at me. When I slept — if I slept — I dreamed about my mother, which must have been Becky's fault, for telling me all those things Aunt Maggie had told her about Mum; I hadn't wanted to hear exactly, but I couldn't stop myself listening, no more I couldn't stop myself thinking about it afterward.

Aunt Maggie had quoted some stupid poem to Becky, for instance, about two baby bears living in a wood. "One of them was bad" — this poem went — "And one of them was good. And then quite suddenly, just like us, one of them got better and the other got wuss ..."

Aunt Maggie had gotten better in their case, Aunt Maggie had announced rather sadly. Whereas her sister, Megan, my mother, had gotten worse. And never gotten no better; in fact she'd ended up by running away and the rest of it. I was getting worse too, I thought. I spent my time grumping and grouching, not speaking nicely to no one, except Zakky Thompson, while Becky grew more friendly not to say pleasant by the day. The only time I spoke nicely was when I was playing Buttons, and goodness knows how he managed to stay friendly — he hadn't a hope in the world. Some Prince called Deirdre Smith was turning up any day to steal his Cinders, plus, no doubt, everything else he'd ever wanted in his life.

On Thursday that week, as promised, our class took the little train to Matlock Bath. First we walked all along the river to the Mining Museum under its great dome. Neither Becky nor me was very keen on that, for one reason and another. When some people insisted on climbing up inside those narrow shafts, we glanced at each other sideways. It's amazing how quickly, I thought, you and another person can get to have the same thoughts no one else knows about. You don't even have to like the person. Becky and I didn't like each other, often. But we knew what each other was thinking and even feeling sometimes, and we both knew then why we was exchanging meaning glances with one another.

The cable car was better. It would have been better still without Class 3Z mucking about whenever the teachers — Mr. Peters, wearing a stupid green bomber jacket, and a geography teacher called Miss Binns I hadn't much noticed before — wasn't looking. Each car had three little separate glass cabins. The downward car slowed when it reached the platform of the station at the bottom, and the doors opened to let people off. But it didn't stop. All the time one lot of people was getting off and the next lot was getting on, the car kept trundling slowly round its little platform. As soon as it reached the end, and the front cabin was facing back the way it came, the doors closed, the car took up speed, was off upward again.

Since all this meant you had to get onto the thing quickly, not stopping to think about it, some dumb clucks was so busy arguing about who they was going with and whether they was going in the back cabin or the front one that they missed the car the first time round.

I wasn't arguing, however, and I didn't get left behind. I went in the middle cabin with Zakky and Becky and Jill Jennings and Tracy Kent — we made a weird-looking group, I tell you.

"The long and the short of it, I presume," Mr. Peters had said once, seeing Zakky and me together. Today, at the sight of Jill and Tracy, he threw his hands in the air, groaned, and asked, "Is one of you heading to be in at the birth and the other at the death, then? I give up."

The fact was that though he'd told us to dress sensibly *please,* we didn't have to wear school clothes for our outing. Tracy had taken "sensibly" to mean giving the white face and purple lipstick a miss, otherwise going as near punk as she dared to; that was a pretty long way for Matlock. Under a black leather, studded jacket, and chain belt borrowed from her brother — so she said — she wore a black sweater, skintight black pants, and black boots, very shiny. Her short hair was spiky with wet-look gel, her eyes rimmed with black liner.

Jill, on the other hand, had rimmed her eyes with pale-blue liner. She wore a powder-pink padded jacket above tight baby-blue jeans and flashy white boots, also shiny. It wasn't hard to see what Mr. Peters meant by "in at the birth" nor "in at the death" neither.

In the cable car Jill and Tracy, of course, did most of the talking. "Well, well, Trace," Jill Jennings said straight off. "Aren't we lucky, here we are with t' stars themselves, Cinderella and Buttons. Got your pen ready to sign autographs, Cinders, have you? What a shame we haven't got Prince Charming in t' car also."

"Why should I need Prince Charming when I've got the Fairy Godmother?" said Becky, who seemed to have taken courage from having Zakky and me on either side. Both Jill and Tracy thought this very funny. They slapped each other's backs and cackled with laughter. "Don't forget t' Angel Gabriel," Tracy said, staring at Zakky, whose nickname it was. But he stared right back amiably like he didn't care a damn. "Aren't you t' lucky one then, Cinders, a Fairy Godmother *and* t' bloody Angel Gabriel. What's your wish then, let us grant it. I know, you don't have to tell us, you'd like to lose that fat bum of yours, wouldn't you, without trying."

Becky gazed out the window and didn't answer. I gazed out the window too. It was like a spaceship, I thought, that glass bubble, it went straight up like a spaceship, making only a faint humming sound. If you looked back and down you could forget about the wire holding it up. One minute you was a midget at the foot of a tall limestone cliff, the next you'd grown so fast you could see over the top of it. It made me feel a bit like Alice after her neck grew long in that book, *Alice in Wonderland,* that my mum kept on reading to me at one time.

The leaves on the trees at the top of the cliff we'd

topped, the leaves on the trees in the wide country beyond it was red and yellow and orange now. Some trees had hardly no leaves left.

Halfway up the steep slope of the cliff in front of us, the Heights of Abraham, the cable car stopped still for a little, so you could take pictures if you had a camera. None of us did. We sat perched like birds above copper-leaved trees — beech trees, I think, I'm beginning to learn the names of some things. Between us and the world below us there wasn't nothing now but air. We could see the river directly below, and the little canoe gates on it and even some canoeists turning what looked like little white feathers of water from their prows and their paddles. Alongside the river a train went down the line to Derby as silent as the canoes seen from where we was, and only a little larger. But I wanted it smaller still and smaller, in the end to vanish altogether. What was the point, I thought, of having all that open air around you and being so locked up you might as well be underground? I wanted to dematerialize through those glass walls, I wanted to lift off into space like Superman.

Or else, I thought, the whole cable car could take off with all of us in it. We could form a new colony in space the way they did in some books. Perhaps on the whole we'd better not, though, I thought, looking around me. A right funny colony we'd make, me and Becky, black-from-head-to-foot Tracy, baby-pink-and-blue Jill, and our wingless Angel Gabriel, Zakky Thompson.

Zakky had his eyes shut, I saw. I wouldn't have put it past him to be praying. He wore a blue jacket with a green stripe across it. Pinned close to the collar was a little red button that said "Jesus Lives." Pinned to his chest was a blue-and-white button that said "Jesus Saves." Anyone would think, I thought, that for all his belief in heaven Zakky hadn't got no head for heights.

Becky's eyes, though, was wide open. She looked excited. She said, "Suppose the wires broke? I often wonder."

"Lost your glass slipper then, have you, Cinderella?" inquired Tracy, leaning forward. "Don't say you're afraid of heights."

"Of course I'm not," said Becky indignantly. "Are you?"

"Don't worry," I said. "If the wires break Zakky will ask Jesus to catch us, won't you, Zakky?" I was getting at Zakky. He annoyed me today, with his red and blue Jesus buttons. But Zakky didn't seem to mind. He didn't even open his eyes. He said, "Jesus could catch us if he wanted. But he mightn't want to. He might think we were sinners and deserved to die."

"He might think we were angels ready to go to heaven," Tracy said, giggling.

"He might," said Zakky, taking her seriously. Or maybe not. As usual it was impossible to tell.

"We're all going to die in the end, aren't we, what's it matter," I said, shrugging my shoulders.

"I'll put R.I.P. on your tombstone if you like, Titch," said Jill Jennings, also giggling. "Rest in Peace."

I saw Becky looking at me. Did she think this wasn't no suitable subject for me, one way and another? It's true it made me think of my mother; was she resting in peace after abandoning me to my fate? I wondered. But much more I was thinking of the boy who cried in my room all night — had *his* mother rested in peace after abandoning him in the mine, all those years ago? She shouldn't have. "R.I.P. if you're lucky," I insisted. "Only if you're very lucky." At the same time, I knew at last, thanks to Jill Jennings of all people, exactly what the ghost wanted. "Bury me" meant he wanted to rest in peace. R.I.P. But how to?

At this very instant, fortunately, the cable car jerked and went on again. So that was that, for the moment.

All through lunch, under tall beech trees, sitting on rocks or wooden seats, Mr. Peters lectured us. On how lucky we were, for instance, what lazy little so-and-sos, two hundred years ago, at the same age and much younger, we'd've walked the whole way up in the dark, at six o'clock every morning, and worked all day in the dark and come out in the dark, with just a crust of bread to our dinners. Whereas just look at us lot, stuffing chips and ham sandwiches and apple pies and Coke, and all kinds of other junk into our overindulged stomachs, *and* without one stroke of work to earn it. (Actually Mr. Peters wasn't doing too badly himself, sharing what looked like a homemade pork pie with Miss Binns, who was very pretty, I noticed, and seemed to like him enough to sit quite close to him, snaky as he was, and offer him cups of coffee out of her thermos.)

He made me think, though, in ways I'd rather not have been thinking. All the way down the hill on the way to the mine afterward, I thought about one of those underfed kids in particular. The kid who hadn't never come out some dark night all those years ago. Who hadn't seen sky ever again, not even a dark one, and who kept me awake of nights with his crying, because of it.

"I don't know why you want burying," I told him. "You're buried already, ain't you, like my mum, like my dad, too, whoever he was, for all I know it."

I don't know what I was expecting the mine to be like. In fact it looked like any other cave I'd been in lately, with concrete steps, low, dripping tunnels, and echoing chambers. There wasn't no stalactites, sadly, and the guide made fewer jokes than the one at Castleton. He told us practical things instead, like the fact that you got stuff to make toothpaste and so forth out of the lead mines now rather than lead, and that lead was poisonous, it destroyed your brain cells if you sucked or smelled too much of it.

("I can think of a few, not too far from here, don't need no lead to eat up their brain cells, didn't have none to start with," I heard Tracy Kent whisper to Jill Jennings. "So can I," I said. "Cheeky," they answered. Perhaps it was too dark for them to notice I wasn't smiling.)

I don't know what I thought was going to happen. Maybe I never imagined anything would. Or maybe I imagined something like last time. Only it wasn't like that, not even when the guide led us aside from the main cavern we had reached into a tall tunnel and then into an alcove in the tunnel. Over our head, high up, at the level where the floor of the cave used to be before the miners dug it out, another tunnel led into the rock. Crouched on a ledge near the entrance to the tunnel was what looked like the figure of a man. The light was so dim I thought he was real at first, and so did the others. But the man didn't move. He had to be a waxwork or something. Meanwhile the guide was saying, "You'll hear someone else talking to you now, but I won't say who 'tis, you'll 'ave to guess when you 'ear 'im."

I saw Becky turn and look at me for some reason. At this moment all the lights went out, leaving us in the pitch dark.

"Now you know," the guide said — some stupid kids was giving little shrieks, of course, clutching at each other, while others was making growls and catcalls hoping to frighten us — "Now you know what it must 'ave felt like fer those miners."

For myself I didn't mind the darkness so much this time, funnily. In fact I was almost disappointed when, above our heads, little flickering lights came on here and there, and sounds of clinking and hammering, dull thuds and echoes, started to resound all round us. You could see shapes of more wax men behind the wax man at the front of the tunnel. I suppose it was meant to show us what it would be like working so far down, with just the little flickering lights in the darkness, with the sounds of picks and things, but it didn't. It wasn't real. It didn't help me imagine how it must have been for my boy in those days. The only thing real was how cold I suddenly felt; icy, right through to my bones — to the marrow, as books are always saying.

"It's just some crummy tape," I heard some-one — Dean Onslow? — exclaim disgustedly when a deep Derbyshire voice started up from above our heads, explaining the day's work they was supposed to have been doing. A moment later it started calling — or pretending to call. "Ned? Ned? Where's that dratted lad, now, coom on, Ned lad, where's us snap, it's dinner time, where thi got to. 'E's niver there when you want him, that lad," the voice confided in us. "'E's going to get left down behind here one of these days. 'E's never here when you want 'im."

Another lost lad then? Possibly. But if I was shivering it was for other reasons, not because of no voice on a tape played so often you could hear the faint hiss in it. Even when the sounds got louder and more urgent it was still only a tape, I knew it. The man was yelling for the lad now, telling him to get out of the way, get a move on, mind out, they was setting explosives in the rock, it'd be the death of him if he didn't, he'd either be blown to pieces like the stone, or trapped behind a rockfall.

(Was that what happened to my boy, then? I wondered. Could it not have been his mother's fault after all? Could *he* have been trapped behind a rockfall?)

I shut my eyes at the sound of the hollow boom that followed. The scrapings and tumblings of rock went on and on, getting nearer and nearer. I doubt if no hunk of rock did hit me on the head, but it felt as if one did. As I swooned and fell I opened my eyes for an instant, could have sworn I saw, behind the bearded waxwork the voice was supposed to be coming from, another much smaller, thinner figure, no waxwork this one; it couldn't have been, it was moving, yet so thin and small it was a flash of bone and skull as much as anything, no more than a scrape, only a scraping of flesh upon it.

My eyes closed again, then. "Will, are you all right, what's t' matter?" a voice said. Another voice added — Tracy? — she sounded accusing — "He fainted." And it's true, when I opened them again I found myself

149

sitting on the ground rather than standing on my feet. The lights was on now. Everyone was standing round me, looking down.

"I bet he's just playing t' fool, as usual," said Tracy, disappointedly. I took my cue from that, clutched my head theatrically — I did feel all right, I realized, apart from my being a bit surprised and still colder than I would have expected — and whispered, even more dramatically, "Didn't you hear the bomb? They blew us up. Didn't you hear them?"

That put them off the track all right, put me off too, which was just what I wanted. I didn't want nothing to do with that skeleton for the moment. Never mind that it meant getting hauled to my feet by Mr. Peters, followed by a nip from his serpent's tooth and hissing tongue for playing silly games. Why should I care? In my head I was whispering at my ghost, "Yes, mate, yes. I saw you. Yes, you convinced me you need help. But I'll help you in my time, not yours. Time's all the same to you, mate, ain't it, but it ain't all the same to me, yet. R.I.P. it is. But it comes in its own time, see, you have to know where to look for it, and I don't know yet, I don't. It's not as if I hadn't looked," I added, remembering Zakky and me poking among the stones at the top of the shaft near Becky's house.

As we came out of the cave Zakky unpinned his blue "Jesus Saves" button and gave it to me. "Do you expect me to wear it?" I asked him. He smiled his lopsided smile and shrugged. "Why not?" he said. "Why not?" I answered, pinning it on my jacket just for the hell of it, next to the CND button and the Women's Rights button given me by my mother.

All the same, Jesus didn't save me. Nor did the fact that Becky and I marched off home that evening heads up, Buttons and his Cinders, cousins against the world, or at least against Jill Jennings and Tracy Kent. That was a comfort. On the other hand, didn't Becky never ask once if I was all right, or what had happened in the cave earlier. She had other things on her mind. I mean it was Guy Fawkes's night that night, no less, her dad had made a bonfire in the garden and Aunt Maggie had bought a box or two of fireworks. Becky and I had made a scarecrow to burn. She couldn't seem to think of nothing except what kind of hat we was going to give him.

In the end we didn't quite dare steal an old hat of Uncle Jim's, let alone Aunt Maggie's. Becky wouldn't give up a striped woolen cap she had neither, though it was too small for her, almost. We made him a cocked hat, like Napoleon's, out of newspaper instead. We'd also stuffed him with newspaper; you'd have thought he'd have burned easily, but he didn't seem to.

"What have you put in that guy of yours, a fire extinguisher?" said Uncle Jim, in a jollier mood than usual, as we stood looking up at the guy's misshapen limbs and body, at his grinning mask face topped by our newspaper hat. By which he meant, I suppose, that though the fire was already blazing, the guy still sat there stiffly, not one licking flame took his body, his mask, his hat. I knew what he must have felt like; it was the same with me exactly. No matter how close I got to it the fire felt cold to me — I couldn't stop shivering.

"Are you all right, Will?" Aunt Maggie asked once, in an anxious whisper, pulling me aside so that no one else would hear her. Of course I told her yes, because I was, in any normal manner of speaking, and even if I wasn't in other ways, I preferred not to try explain it.

It wasn't nothing to do with the bonfire, neither. We cooked potatoes in it, they cooked all right, they was hot in my mouth when we ate them. I suppose the guy burned in the end too, no one said no more about it, and one time I looked up he wasn't there no longer, though I never saw him burn, only saw the flames licking uselessly about him. The flames had licked round me, too, as I'd pulled the potatoes out of the embers. But my fingers didn't burn, or at least I didn't notice them burning. My hands inside my gloves stayed frozen as ever.

I went to bed cold that night too. Even Soldier wouldn't come to my bed to warm me. It was one of those nights — there'd been several lately — when he stood at my door, looking guilty, his tail thumping,

refusing to come no farther. In the morning I awoke still
cold, after dreaming all night of a set of bones curled up,
as if asleep, in a rock tunnel. I'd found myself begging
them, over and over, "Please leave me alone. Please
leave me alone. I know what you want, but I just
can't help. Well, I will in the end, but now I don't
know how to."

# 11

## BECKY

The morning after bonfire night, I woke up frozen. The whole house was cold, I discovered when I went downstairs to breakfast. All through our cornflakes and bacon, Dad kept on shouting at us loudly.

"Now then, own up, who did it? I locked that front door as usual before I went to bed. I chained it. I bolted it." Mum and Will and I looked at each other blankly. Mum said soothingly, "But you can't have done, dear. It was wide open when I came down. Judging by the cold it had been open most of the night."

"Then someone must have opened it. Who was it? Becky? Will?"

But I hadn't opened the front door. To judge by his face, Will hadn't done so either, though I'm sure they thought it was him. When he still didn't own up, they had to accept his word for it. What else could they do, Will being the way he was, my mother seeing him the way she did; this wasn't a hundred miles off the way I saw him, I could guess, now I'm older.

In the end we assumed it was some stupid mistake and forgot all about it. But it happened a second time.

And a third. Mum and Dad started getting suspicious of each other. Dad made Mum look on each night while he bolted and chained the door and locked it. But still, two or three times at least over the next few weeks we found bolts undone, the chain hanging, the key turned when we came downstairs in the morning. I always knew which mornings too, almost before I got out of bed. I woke up so cold those mornings, yet I hadn't gone to sleep cold, not as I remembered.

Almost the worst thing was that no one had a clue what to do about it. I heard Mum and Dad arguing one day — Dad said he would call the police; Mum said what was the point, nothing had been stolen.

"But it will be, the door wide open all those nights," Dad said. "It's got to stop." He shouted this. I agreed with him that it had to, it was all really creepy. They noticed me then and they didn't go on with the conversation, but my mother must have persuaded Dad to wait a bit longer, because the police didn't come. I bet she was afraid they'd accuse Will and upset him.

I had my own suspicions of Will too, I have to tell you, even though I couldn't see how he could have gotten downstairs without one of us hearing, the floors in our house creaking the way they do. I used to hear him fetching up Soldier sometimes, and twice I went down after he'd come back to look at the front door. It wasn't open then, either time. But the second time I looked, it was open the next morning.

Once I even accused Will to his face of doing it. He looked so terrified and wretched, I wished I hadn't. What's more, it occurred to me just then that he might be doing it without knowing, and perhaps that was what he was so afraid of. Perhaps it explained the weird way he was behaving at the moment.

"Perhaps it's me — I'm sleepwalking and I don't know it," I said, to mollify him a little.

"I doubt it," he answered, shaking his head.

"You don't think it was your ghost," I said jokingly, and then I wasn't joking anymore, I was frightened for a minute. Even though Will's ghost, the one he heard, never seemed to have had much to do with me.

It could have been I was most frightened by Will being so frightened.

"I haven't got a ghost," he shouted.

"But Will, you told me . . . What about the crying . . . ?"

"You don't have to believe everything I say, do you?" he said, his face white with anger.

"What about the photograph, Will? What about the fruit?"

He didn't say anything. He just looked at me. As if the fruit at least was all my fault.

He had me in tears now, almost. Not just because of what he'd said, but because of the way everything was going wrong between us. At one point I could have almost believed he was my real brother; not any longer, not the way he was getting further and further away from me. The only time he seemed like the old Will was when he was playing Buttons. Then he fooled about like he always had done, at the same time so sadly, pathetically, it was enough to make me want to weep, or else to bash him over the head for being so stupid.

Not that I lost much sleep over it — though afterward, seeing what happened, I thought I ought to have worried more about him. Nothing, not Will, not the ghost, if there was one, not the way the door kept on flying open in the night, could worry me for long while I was being Cinderella. Being Cinderella was the best thing that had happened to me in my life, better than anything in my old school even. Why should I care who left a silly old door open? Why, almost, should I care about my cousin behaving so oddly? Indeed, why should I care when Tracy Kent and Jill Jennings said I couldn't sing for toffee (and it's true that singing "Some Day My Prince Will Come" by myself or "Whistle a Happy Tune" with Will wasn't the best of it) so long as Mr. Peters seemed to think it was all right. All I cared about was being the best Cinderella ever, about hearing Mr. Peters or Miss Binns — but I'd sooner it was Mr. Peters — say, "Well done, Becky, that's coming along nicely."

Miss Binns was the coproducer of our pantomime now. She seemed to like Mr. Peters very much, almost as much as Mr. Peters seemed to like her. I was quite jealous really. Every day that went by I liked Mr. Peters better. So did all the other girls in the class, it seemed to me. Everyone was much keener to wipe the blackboard for him, or tidy up his pen-and-paper drawer, or fetch his coffee from the staff room during rehearsals, than they had been for Mr. Carlson, the teacher we'd had in the second year.

Jill Jennings liked Mr. Peters too, I noticed. At least she seemed to like him during our rehearsals — she cheeked him back the way I'd never dared to. She was even quite nice to me, sometimes, when we had a scene together. This was another thing I'd noticed, that neither she nor Tracy Kent was quite so bad when you got them on their own. Together, though, they egged each other on to say nasty things, to try and make everyone in the class laugh at your singing or your fat bottom, or the fact that you'd been at a private school before.

I told my mother about them one day when we were drinking tea in the kitchen after school — I didn't mind telling her about such things now they didn't upset me quite so much. She said, "They sound a proper double act. Me and Megan were a double act, when we weren't fighting that is."

Will was having tea with us too. He didn't say anything, as usual, but as usual I noticed how he drank up every word my mother said about his mother.

"Did you use to fight a lot?" I asked her.

"Oh yes. All over the floor sometimes. In the end people were complaining; they had to put us in a different class."

"Did you mind being put in a different class?"

"I didn't. In a way I quite liked it. That was the time Megan seemed to be better at everything than I was. But Megan hated it. She hated me for not minding. Come to think, it was after that she started getting thin. I think people teased her when I wasn't there to stop them."

Will's getting thin, I thought, staring at him across the table. As if he could get any thinner; he'd been like a beanpole to start with. I saw my mother looking at him too. She was worried about him, I know. She'd told me. She'd asked me once if I knew what was the matter. I said I didn't, not in particular. My mother and I were getting on so well those days, I half thought of saying, "He thinks he keeps hearing a ghost," but found I couldn't, though it would have been a relief if I could have, if we'd been able to worry about it together. For one thing Will had sworn to me he wasn't hearing a ghost. For another I thought she might think he was crazy, and then other people might, then they might take him away from us again, put him in a hospital or something. I didn't think he was crazy. And besides, I didn't want him leaving us again, even if he wasn't much company for the moment.

My mother and I weren't the only ones worried about Will, either. Mr. Peters was worried about him. Ms. Simms, the social worker, seemed to be worried about him too. She came up to see Will one day. I walked into the kitchen to find her and my mother with their heads together talking about him in low and anxious-sounding voices. The problem was that Will wasn't doing any wrong exactly, apart from opening the front door at night, if it was him, and still no one had proved it. He was getting up in the morning and going to school and coming home again and doing his homework — well, most of it, anyway. It would have been easier to do something about it if he was making a nuisance of himself. But he wasn't.

Ms. Simms had a long talk with Will — or rather she talked. He didn't say anything. Afterward she shrugged her shoulders, said something to my mother about trying Child Guidance if things didn't improve, and went back to London. My father had altogether stopped trying to talk to him about football or anything else. As for Mr. Peters, he told Will where he should stand, where he should sit, when he should move, and when he should stop still for Buttons, and that was it.

In fact the only people who hadn't given up on him entirely were my mother and me and Zakky Thompson. Zakky still went around with Will all the time, though I hardly heard them say a word to one another. Even my mother, as I said, was reduced to asking my advice.

As for me, the reason I hadn't given up on him was because the way he was as Buttons often made me want to weep.

It was one rehearsal, in particular, that made me realize what I felt. It was getting toward the end of term already, and we'd moved out of rehearsing in the classroom to rehearsing on the stage in the school hall. Of course, we didn't have the scenery up, and we were all wearing our own clothes, but we had some of the props we needed — I had my broom to lean on, for instance. I seemed to spend my life as Cinderella leaning on a broom when I wasn't sweeping the floor with it. Also our voices sounded hollow in all that space, the way they hadn't when we were rehearsing in the classroom; Mr. Peters kept on shouting at us "to speak up," "to project ourselves" — otherwise no one at the back of the hall was going to hear us.

Miss Binns was playing the piano for the songs that day. Mr. Peters spent most of his time leaning against the piano and sometimes leaning down to talk to her, to point to some bit of music, his cheek much nearer to her cheek than it need have been. It made me feel a bit funny seeing that. It made Jill Jennings feel a bit funny too, judging by the way she was looking at them. We caught each other's eye at that point. I could have sworn that Jill Jennings, of all people, blushed. She didn't make a single nasty remark, either. She just looked away and that was that.

The last but one scene in the play, when I said good-bye to Buttons and the Fairy Godmother appeared to bless me and Deirdre Smith/Prince Charming (why didn't Buttons get a blessing too? I wondered, but it never seemed to be in the story), was a particularly soppy one. Mr. Peters had written the script for the pantomime. Some of it was quite funny, because of the Ugly Sisters and so forth, and because it made all sorts of jokes about the school and the other teachers. But this scene wasn't funny at all. After Dean Onslow and Neil Bright, the Ugly Sisters, had exited, pretending to faint from shock because Prince Charming wanted to marry Cinderella rather than them (who could blame her) and Prince Charming had gone off to fetch his coach, Buttons had to hold out his hands to me and say:

> *"Once my heart was light as a feather,*
> *You and I, Cinders, had such lovely times together.*
> *But now who's going to love poor Buttons?*
> *Not your Ugly Sisters for sure, those gluttons,*
> *Shouting bring us breakfast, idle boy,*
> *Clean our slippers, hobbledehoy.*
> *That'll be my life from now on,*
> *My heart is broken, dear little Cinders is gone."*

And then I had to say:

> *"Don't you remember our song, dear friend,*

162

*Let's sing it again together, don't let this be an end."*

And we sang a verse of "Whistle a Happy Tune" while
Buttons slowly began a funny dance, which he'd still
be dancing — still whistling — when I went off on the
arm of Deirdre Smith/Prince Charming. But then I had
to pause on the edge of the stage and look back, and
he'd have stopped dancing and whistling, he'd be crying
with his head in his hands. Or pretending to cry.

I don't know what it was that day in particular.
Maybe it was something about us being on the proper
stage, with the lights on, and the rest of the hall
stretching away dimly, so that the stage itself seemed
the only real life, so that even those silly words meant
more than anything we could have said in our own
persons. But the moment Will started to say them
he looked so genuinely wretched, he broke my heart.
I could hardly whistle a single note. Only an hour before
he'd been unfriendly and strange enough to make me
hate him and wonder what the point was of having
a cousin if you weren't able to say one word without
having your head bitten off; in fact I'd wondered how
anyone so weird and dark and foreign-looking could be
my cousin in the first place. Now, seeing his sadness
as the jilted Buttons, he didn't look foreign to me at
all. He looked like my black-haired cousin. I wanted to
run back to him, fling my arms round him, anything
to stop him looking so unhappy. I'd never felt that

way about anyone else's unhappiness before, not even my mother's sadness over Megan. I'd never in my life wanted to look after and protect anyone or anything except a guinea pig I'd had when I was little, and that hadn't lasted long — after a week or two my mother had fed it.

"Becky," Mr. Peters shouted at me suddenly from his place by the piano, "you're supposed to be looking happy. It's Prince Charming you're supposed to be in love with, not Buttons, remember?"

Everyone sitting watching in the hall or at the back of the stage burst out laughing then. "Incest, incest," a voice hissed behind me — Jill Jennings, of course. That was the big joke in our class when anyone seemed really to like their brother and sister, or at least didn't pretend they didn't like them. "Incest, incest."

But Will wasn't my brother. He was my cousin. And anyway it wasn't like that.

That night, as it happened, I noticed the oddest thing. We were sitting by the fire in the sitting room. Will in particular was huddled close up to it, so close you'd think his skin would be scorching.

"You'll burn yourself if you get any closer, Will," I said.

"No I won't," he answered. And it was true, he didn't look scorched. His cheek wasn't getting red and blotchy the way I felt mine was. Curious, I reached out and put a hand on his cheek, and to my amazement it not only didn't look hot, it *wasn't* hot. It felt cold to my finger. Waxy. Like the skin of a dead person, or how I imagined the skin of a dead person would feel.

It was getting near Christmas now. People were growing excited. I was excited. My mother would arrive back from shopping around the time we arrived back from school, laden with parcels that she took upstairs and hid. At school you heard carols coming out of every room as classes practiced for the carol concert that always followed the pantomime. There were paper chains up in all the corridors and a big Christmas tree in the hall alongside the stage. Underneath it was a growing heap of colored parcels, presents for an old people's home in the next parish.

We didn't have a Christmas tree at home yet. It was a tradition in our family that it would be standing in the hall when I got home from school on the last day of term. My mother said that even that was much earlier for a Christmas tree than she'd been used to when she was a child. (She nearly said "me and Megan," but something about Will seemed suddenly to have stopped her mentioning Megan all the time, making up for all the years, I suppose, that she had never mentioned Megan ever. The only trouble with my dear mother was that she made it so obvious she was about to say "Megan," then prevented herself in a hurry, that she might as well not have bothered.) Then, she said, they'd never had a tree till Christmas Eve. In fact when she was very small she'd go to sleep on Christmas Eve and wake up on Christmas morning to see the decorated tree for the first time, with her Christmas stocking beneath it.

I think Christmas must have been magical like that. At the same time I really liked the way we did it. Each year when I arrived home on the last school afternoon with my bags of school junk that I didn't have to look at again for three whole weeks, I'd find the ordinary, not very friendly, hall light replaced by the soft glitter of little white gilded lights strung over the Christmas tree and reflected in the gold and silver, red, blue, and green glass balls strung from its boughs. Each year it made me feel Christmas had very nearly come.

We didn't have a star or a fairy at the top of our tree. Instead, jammed against the low hall ceiling stood a fine glass peacock flaunting its glass tail; that glorious green and blue and golden spread of his glass tail promised Christmas, all of it, in all its glitter and glory. In fact he was better than Christmas, the way it often turned out. He was splendid; I loved him. For weeks and weeks this year I found myself longing for him, thinking exultantly, I feel like a peacock, I know what he feels like, raised on a stage above everyone else. I *am* Cinderella.

Perhaps Will being so funny to me wasn't strange after all. Maybe my being so pleased with myself, even a bit conceited during those weeks, was enough to make anyone turn funny.

Three Saturdays before Christmas, the Saturday before the pantomime, my mother took us both shopping at the Eagle Center in Derby. There was a Santa Claus in the department store. Of course we were much too old to go and sit on his knee and be asked what we wanted in our stockings, but I regretted it a little. There was tinsel and holly in all the shop windows and Christmas carols playing in the shopping mall. I hummed "God Rest Ye Merry Gentlemen" to myself as I went through the science fiction shelves in Smith's, wishing I knew for sure which ones Will had read. In fact I spent most of the day buying presents for Will, what with one thing and another. Apart from finding my own present for him, I had to help my mother choose things for his Christmas stocking — in whispers, of course, when Will wasn't looking. It made me feel more pleased than ever that he was spending Christmas with us. I felt that once he'd had Christmas with us then he really would be part of our family. I knew now for certain I wanted him to be part of our family.

I suppose Will had been buying presents. He spent most of the time in Smith's, and most of that around the bookshelves. He carried home some parcels wrapped in white-and-orange Smith's paper.

In the hall, when I dumped everything down I

167

knocked my purse onto the floor and all my money came tumbling out. I meant to pick it up at once, but my mother was yelling at me to come and help her make the tea and so I didn't.

In fact I thought no more about it until we were sitting in the kitchen peacefully drinking our tea and eating crumpets and Eccles cakes we'd bought from Marks and Spencers, the two dogs sitting by our feet and looking up at us hopefully. Even my mother seemed less anxious and tired than she usually did just before Christmas, than she had done lately every time she looked at Will. Before we sat down she had not only given me a little hug, she'd half given Will one too before he'd time to dodge. But then, quite suddenly, my father burst in through the door, yelling. He didn't usually yell like that. I mean swearing. The words I'm not allowed to say in front of him. Maybe the ever-open front door had been getting at him or something; he seemed really shaken this time, really upset. I suppose you would feel like that if things kept happening for which there was no explanation and you were the kind of person who expected explanations for everything, even your own near-bankruptcy, like my father.

Apart from the swear words, what he was yelling was incomprehensible stuff about jokers and last straws and vandals. He was looking straight at Will. I'm sure he suspected Will of all kinds of things those days, not just door opening. Apart from having given up trying to talk boys' talk to him about football and things, he looked at Will very oddly sometimes, though he never said anything. But what he was shouting about now couldn't have had anything to do with Will. Will had been crouched on the floor stroking Soldier when I came into the room. He hadn't been out of my sight since I'd knocked my purse onto the hall floor, a hundred years ago it felt like, or just this minute.

An old oak chest stood directly under the window in the hall in those days. As soon as we followed my father out there we could feel the cold wind drilling its way through the broken pane above it. The glass shards from the pane were laid almost neatly on the wooden chest. On the floor below, as if blown there by the wind, all the coins in my purse, brown ones, silver ones, one yellow pound coin, had formed themselves into words, two words, on the red hall carpet. Rather shaky and misshapen words, yet still unmistakable. BURY ME, they read.

# 12

## W I L L

It was the first time in weeks I'd wanted to laugh aloud, seeing their faces when they came across the words BURY ME written in coins on the hall floor. Such words couldn't frighten me that way, not no longer. I'd heard them whispered in my ear endlessly, day and night. In fact they was the least of the things I'd had to put up with lately; the footsteps echoing mine wherever I went in the house; the doors that I hadn't laid no hand on opening or shutting behind or in front of me; the cold flames of the fire in the grate. Like the bonfire flames that ought to have been hot that they froze me; I couldn't get warm no matter how close to them I got myself.

Becky wasn't the only one to discover that strange thing neither. Aunt Maggie touched my hand once when I was huddled by the fire. The same look came on her face then as came on Becky's, and I can't blame them for it. Who wouldn't look strange finding the skin of one practically burning himself in the fire as cold as ice? Aunt Maggie persuaded herself I must be sickening for something. She took my temperature and though I hadn't no fever — the reverse — she kept me from school next day and fed me hot honey and lemon. That was nice, in fact. My mother used to give me hot honey and lemon when I was ill, at least I seem to remember she did.

Nothing else was nice. Like I said, the boy never let me alone; soon as I walked into the house he'd be waiting. There was going to be no R.I.P. for me, certain, not until I'd found some kind of R.I.P. for him.

And still I didn't feel ready to help him, I don't know why. Perhaps I was even more afraid of going down into the dark than I was afraid of him. Perhaps I knew he wasn't as dangerous as that narrow shaft, those rocks, that darkness.

I thought I might know where to find him. I went up to the shaft above Knob Farm quite often; not during the week, there wasn't no time after school before it got dark, nor was there time in the early morning. Because of his keeping me awake so much at night with his whisperings and screamings, his proddings and twitching, like a younger brother forced to share my bed, it was morning sometimes before I got to sleep at all; Aunt Maggie had great difficulty in dragging me out from under the flowery duvet in time to catch the school bus. No, I went there on Saturdays and Sundays with Zakky. We'd succeeded in digging out some of the stones. We thought it wouldn't take much more to find the shaft, but somehow we never did. I don't think either of us quite wanted to. Well, I didn't. Once I said, "Think of all that dark down there."

Zakky replied, as if he was quoting, "Jesus shall be a light unto our darkness."

"I thought you'd promised only to talk about Jesus on Sundays," I said.

"So I had," he agreed amiably.

"Do you really believe all that stuff, Zakky?"

"Why shouldn't I believe it?" he said. "Wouldn't you like to?"

"Not much," I said. "My mum believed some of it once. It didn't help her."

"The Lord moves in mysterious ways," said Zakky, which was one of the few times I really wanted to hit him. What could he know about my mum? How dare he?

"There wasn't no mystery about what happened to my mum," I said. "Hadn't you better be off home now? I didn't invite you to tea, did I?"

The funny thing was I felt bad about that afterward. There was something so harmless about Zakky. Well, no, not harmless, not even innocent; just straight up and down. At the same time, with his buttons, and his long, thin nose, his straight hair cut so short it was bristles on the back of his neck, his long, thin legs and stooped shoulders, he was the most mysterious person I had ever met — like the Angel Gabriel in a way, his namesake. He had a voice like the Angel Gabriel too, I'd discovered, now that we was rehearsing for the Christmas carols as well as the pantomime.

Christmas! How I hated the thought of it. It made me think of Mum all over again. She was the only person I wanted to buy a present for, and the only one there was no point buying nothing for.

That first day shopping I just ended up with two science fiction books for myself, plus a diary for Ms. Simms. Aunt Maggie gave me the money; it had to be sent off soon, otherwise it wouldn't reach her for Christmas.

As for the rest of it, the paper chains and the parcels and the school Christmas tree and the carols, it made me so angry I wanted to pull that Christmas tree down myself, like Samson pulled down the pillars of the temple in a Bible story Zakky told me.

The pantomime was all right. The pantomime was the only thing that was all right. I liked being Buttons. I felt sorry for him. He was like my ghost in a way, except that playing him I was his mind master, in control of him the way I wasn't in control of the ghost. You could say the ghost was my mind master these days. He came to me anytime he wanted, pulling the plug out and emptying my bath of water, rattling my window, driving Soldier and Sailor away — neither of them wouldn't hardly come near my room now, no matter how I tried to bribe them with bits of chocolate and even meat I stole once from a stew Aunt Maggie was making.

In fact the only thing I didn't like about the pantomime was the way Becky mooned after Mr. Peters. Though I knew all the other girls had a crush on him, I'd expected her to have more sense. (I bet none of them would have noticed him like that, neither, if he hadn't started mooning after the geography teacher, Miss Binns.)

The pantomime and the carol concert was to be on the last day of the Christmas term. Unlike everybody else, I wasn't looking forward to the holidays. Once term finished there wouldn't be nothing but the kid and me, I wouldn't be able to escape him, ever. I worried about it all the time. I didn't need no ghost to keep me awake of nights no longer, I kept myself awake, sweating over him. It was as if the little bastard knew that too. He didn't bother me so much that last week, even the fire learned how to warm me some days. This was just as well, since it was getting colder by the minute. There wasn't no leaves on the trees no longer, the trees was gray, the sky was gray, the hills and fields was gray. I didn't know where to look to avoid grayness. But then I didn't want to avoid it, for at the moment I much preferred grayness to color.

But of course at Christmas there was color, lots and lots of it. The shops was the worst with all their frost glitter and colored sparkles, all those banners yelling

Merry Christmas or Happy Yuletide. But how could anyone be merry or happy without no mother for Christmas, with some wretched little ghost thrusting his bones into his head all the time, pestering the life out of him one way or another?

The day of the dress rehearsal, it's true I felt a bit more cheerful. It was good getting into someone else's clothes, even ones that made me look strange, in my opinion. I had a little brown pair of britches to the knee, white stockings underneath, a gilt-buttoned waistcoat, and a big-sleeved white shirt, the front all ruffled. I had a pair of shiny shoes with high heels and gold buckles. Actually they was a pair of my own black shoes, the shine painted, the buckles gold paper, the heels bits of wood cut especially to fit by Dean Onslow's dad and stuck on. And get this for a laugh, Becky thought this load of cobblers suited me. She looked at me like she hadn't never clapped eyes on me before, like she fancied me almost. "That white shirt looks nice with your black hair," she said.

"I can't help who my father was," I told her, and the way she blushed I knew what she'd been thinking. On t'other hand, like this Derbyshire lot would say, why should I care I don't look like I came from the Midlands. We're still cousins, never mind, tough on us, Becks, ain't it?

As for Becky, in the kitchen scenes she wore her hair brushed out and a little ragged brown dress. For the ball Miss Binns put her hair up and puffed powder all over it and attached little false ringlets. Her pink silk ball dress, made out of some old curtains Aunt Maggie had produced from somewhere, had a kind of cage underneath to make the skirt stick out. I thought she looked prettier in the ragged brown dress myself, but she still looked pretty — not even Jill Jennings and Tracy Kent couldn't say she didn't. Under those long dresses no one would see if she had fat legs either, even if she did have.

The only trouble was she looked more and more like my mother now she was so much thinner. I'd have sooner she looked like Aunt Maggie, if I was honest.

Even so, as Buttons, I did my best to win her. I skipped onstage and said:

> "*Cheer up, cheer up my little Cinderella,*
> *Buttons is here, your ever happy fella.*
> *I know that ugly pair your sisters keep getting you down,*
> *I know they never do anything but frown.*
> *If you let Buttons smile for you,*
> *And whistle a happy tune or two,*
> *You'll forget the twisters,*
> *Not care a fig or button for such stupid blisters.*
> *So cheer up, pretty one, cheer up, Cinderella,*
> *Buttons loves you much more than Mr. Sellars.*"

(Mr. Sellars was the headmaster. Mr. Peters got his

name in at every possible moment. It was quite convenient that his name rhymed, more or less, with Cinderella. The deputy headmistress was called Mrs. Addison; he had much more trouble with that. He made one of the Ugly Sisters talk about going to Madison Square Garden — wherever that was — to watch the boxing. Not once but three times. I'm not sure Mr. Peters was really a good poet.)

And so it went on. But it wasn't no use, was it? What could I do against a Prince Charming covered in gold braid, even if he was called Deirdre Smith offstage and was a girl really, even if Becky did think those days that black eyes and hair was worth looking at? Still, the dress rehearsal was all right, on the whole. I didn't mind it. I even enjoyed it. What with all the things that went wrong, the curtains sticking, the scenery falling over, people forgetting their lines or singing flat, with Mr. Peters yelling how useless we all was, and he didn't know why he bothered, none of us ever listened to a word he said, this thing was going to be the worst disaster in the whole history of his school pantomimes, it was hard to get into the part really, it was hard to take Buttons and Prince Charming and Cinderella seriously. Especially when one of the fourth-years who was helping shift scenery leaned over and said loud enough for everyone in the hall to hear, "That's just what old Snake Bite said last year. *And* the year before."

The performance was something different though, entirely.

Maybe it had something to do with us being up there behind the curtains first and then, when the curtains went back (Mr. Peters had gotten Old Grunts, the school caretaker, to climb up and fix them), being shut behind the bright lights. It made me feel I was in another world altogether from the audience down in the dark. I tried not to look at it; it seemed like one great alien animal laughing and sighing and clapping and even singing with us sometimes. Meanwhile, in our bright separate room, up there on the hall stage, I really felt like Buttons. What happened to Buttons was like happening to me. I loved Becky/Cinderella, for instance, I hated her sisters, Dean Onslow and Neil Bright, even more I hated Deirdre Smith/Prince Charming for taking Becky/Cinderella away from me like that Mike took my mother when I was little.

Of course, I didn't hate everything. I enjoyed hearing the audience laugh, for instance, when I dropped trays of milk and coffee all over the Ugly Sisters, or when I tripped up their father, the Baron, or when I turned a somersault over the table, or when I pretended to be scared of the Fairy Godmother (as I might well be scared, seeing it was Jill Jennings — she had a vicious pinch). Or when I danced a jig in front of the curtains with the pumpkin mice, played by two of the smallest girls from the first year, while the pumpkin was being turned into a coach behind the curtains.

Also I liked the coach. The coach was brilliant. Mr. Black, the head of the art and technology department, had made the frame out of light metal; the windows and wheels was offcuts of wood, shaped and fitted together by the woodwork class. The gilded sides and top had been designed and painted by an art class. While Cinderella sat inside, wearing her pink silk dress, three of the boys dressed as horses and prancing so much you wouldn't have thought they could pull nothing dragged it slowly across the stage, to the tune of the triumphal march from "Judas Maccabeus" — "See How the Conquering Hero Comes" (but why not heroine?) — and then the trumpet voluntary played double forte (loudly to you) not only by Miss Binns at the piano but by the school recorder band, a bugler from the local church army band, and two trumpeters and two drummers from the brass band attached to the nearest coal mine. That was fantastic. The audience cheered and so did I. Becky looked great. The music made me want to cry. As far as I was concerned the pantomime went downhill from then on.

By the time the finale came and she swept off on the arm of Prince Charming/Deirdre Smith in his high heels and gold-trimmed coat, to the sound of the Wedding March, Cinderella/Becky had quite forgotten me, I knew. I mean, as she spoke the last few lines I was going to get from her in this story, she didn't hardly bother to look at me even.

> *"I'll not forget you, my old friend,*
> *Never, never, never till I reach my life's end ..."*

Oh yeah, I thought cynically. You've forgotten me already, Cinders baby, you can't even be bothered to clap eyes on me no longer, what price my black hair and white shirt suiting each other now. I hated her. I hated all those faces down there in the dark, the clapping hands making a noise rising and falling, just like the waves of the sea. I thought, I'm antimatter, that's what I am. If antimatter touches matter it explodes. They'll explode. Deirdre and Becky and the audience will explode. The bloody tree will explode. Everything will explode, including me. I *am* antimatter.

As all the cast lined up on the stage behind me ready to take its bow, I began to gaze at the audience, unblinking. Recognizable faces swam up out of the darkness. At about the middle of the hall I saw Aunt Maggie, smiling, applauding vigorously, next to her Uncle Jim swaying about a bit, not smiling.

"Producer, producer," somebody started yelling, and next thing there was Mr. Peters, in one of his golden-brown suits, dragging Miss Binns on as his assistant. She didn't want to come, or pretended not to, but at least it gave her and Old Snaky an excuse to hold each other's hands. After a bit Mr. Peters took

Becky's hand and held up that too — I sneaked a look sideways and saw her beaming as if she hadn't never been so happy in all her life, why should she care if Jill Jennings, her Fairy Godmother, ha-ha, was standing just behind her, poking her viciously with her silver-paper magic wand.

Star of the show, bride of Prince Charming, Mr. Peters holding her hand, of course Becky was happy. Of course she wasn't thinking of me — I was just antimatter. Little did she know, though, how powerful antimatter is, how I could make them all explode, any moment I wanted.

Maybe I would have made them all explode too. Only I looked at the audience suddenly while it was applauding me, and all the time I was taking my bows — even Uncle Jim was clapping now, I saw, at half the speed of everybody else — I imagined myself not as antimatter no longer but as an extraterrestrial being; like E.T. for instance.

As an extraterrestrial being I might look strange to earth people, to these pink Midlands earth people in particular, I thought, staring down at them. But that wasn't nothing to how strange earth people, Midlands people, looked to me. They had moving jelly holes for seeing out of, jutting bits of bone covered in soft stuff for smelling with and slobbering holes full of little white bone for speaking and eating with (eating? What's eating? As an extraterrestrial being I was continually injected with atmospheric vitamin juice). Apart from funny whorled bits of flesh for hearing with, they also had stuff called hair — hair? — what was that fuzzy stuff earthlings wore on top of their heads *for?* Indeed, what was those five-forked brown or pink things the people down there was banging together, making an extraordinary racket, *for?* I wondered.

And from then on, all the time Mr. Peters was making his speech about how he'd enjoyed himself this year, how good we had been, the best group he'd ever had (he'd said that last year too, someone whispered), thanking the headmaster, the technology master, the music master, the art mistress, the caretaker, and so on, I kept seeing the audience with extraterrestrial eyes. Of course, they would have thought I was laughing for the same reason as the rest of the cast, because of Mr. Peters's jokes and so forth. In fact, I was laughing at the funny whorled things on the side of their heads called ears, at the funny stuff on all their earthling heads (why ever *do* we have hair?). Long, short, straight, curly, thin, thick, brown, yellow, gray, even black hair, though none of it as black as mine.

Who knows, it could have been that which stopped antimatter (me) exploding matter (them, and the whole hall, and the Christmas tree — especially the Christmas tree). Or it could have been all the lights going off suddenly, the piano starting up very quietly, and then Zakky Thompson appearing from the back of the hall dressed up in wings and halo — his parents let him dress up as an angel, that was religious — carrying a candle and singing the first verse from "Once in Royal David's City," same as it was always sung in the carol service my mum used to listen to on Christmas Eve, every year, never fail, crying a bit sometimes.

It nearly made me cry now; antimatter, extraterrestrial being, whatever I was. I couldn't have blown nothing or no one up at that moment.

*"Once in Royal David's city,*
*Stood a lowly cattle shed,*
*Where a mother laid her baby,*
*In a manger for his bed  . . ."*

(Lucky baby, I thought.)

Behind Zakky came Tracy Kent dressed in a white tunic, carrying a candle and without a trace of wet-look hair gel or black eyeliner. Maybe I hadn't never mentioned that she too could really sing. Though she'd only been in the pantomime chorus, Mr. Peters had made her sing two solos already. Now she sang the second verse of "Once in Royal David's City" with Zakky, looking as if butter wouldn't melt in her mouth. After her came the choir, all of them carrying candles. All of them sang the next verses processing slowly up the center of the hall. When they reached the front of it they split up; half came up the steps on the right of the stage, half came up on the left, then they was all on the stage with us, Zakky still singing loudest of all, his voice so deep when he spoke, yet singing, pure and strong as a trumpet. I hadn't never heard no one sing like Zakky, before or since. Dressed as yet another kind of extraterrestrial being with his wings and halo, he not only looked like an extraterrestrial being, he sounded just like one.

It started snowing driving home. I liked that. What I did not like was what we found when we opened the front door. You could say it set antimatter meeting matter at last; to put it another way, turned me into a raving madman. I raved. I exploded. There shouldn't be no Christmas tree yet, I was yelling. You shouldn't have no Christmas tree till Christmas Eve, Mum always said, never mind what other people did, that was the way she'd always known it, and that was the way she liked it. That was the way I liked it too. It was the only way things should be done, *ever*.

I didn't put it quite like that. By which I mean I used every word no one did in Aunt Maggie's household, even ones Uncle Jim hadn't used the time he exploded. I stamped as well as bellowed. I wrenched colored balls off the lit-up tree and threw them into splinters. Pretty soon Uncle Jim got hold of me and wrestled my arms behind my back. "Let me go!" I screamed, writhing and struggling.

"Let him go," Aunt Maggie said, pleading with me as much as him.

I don't know whether I listened to her or not. "Please, Will," she was saying, altogether helpless I saw, she didn't know what to do with me, I knew now, no more than my mother never used to, meaning there isn't no one, nowhere, can really be relied on. Even my uncle couldn't hold me more than a minute, apart from his not knowing what to do with me when he had me. But when I'd wriggled out of his grasp I found I'd had the lot of them, I couldn't be bothered no longer. I charged up to my room, slamming the door behind me, then pulled everything down onto the floor, my bedding, my clothes, everything, pushed the empty chest of drawers against the door so no one couldn't open it, though Aunt Maggie tried to.

"Go away!" I screamed. "Go away, leave me alone," again using all my swear words. I did the same to Becky, when she came a bit later. "Suit yourself," she hissed through the crack in the door. "Aren't you a problem?"

I heard Aunt Maggie again later. She was leaving some food there, she said, her voice quite brisk and normal, I must be hungry. But I didn't go out and get it. I lay down on my bed instead, on the bare mattress. Before I knew, not expecting it, I fell fast asleep, to dream of nothing.

When I woke up it was still snowing outside. The snowflakes against the window wove to and fro, glimmering eerily in the snow light that seemed to fill the darkness.

I could see so easily in the kind of light they made that I didn't need to turn the light on as I fumbled on the floor for my warmest clothes. I'm coming, I was telling the voice in my head. I'm coming. At last. Like you wanted. R.I.P.

In a daze, like a sleepwalker more than a waking person, I dragged the duvet across the bed and huddled pillows to make it look as if someone was asleep under it. Then I pulled the chest of drawers away from the door as quietly as I could and went downstairs to find the Christmas tree still lit, its white glitter still filling the hallway. It didn't mean nothing to me no more — though I considered pulling it over, there didn't seem no point in doing so. By the tree's dim light I found the little red flashlight I was looking for in the drawer of the hall table.

Then I went to the front door, pulled back the bolts, unhooked the chain, and turned the key in the bottom lock.

I looked back at the tree as I pulled the door open — the icy blast of wind and cold snow light seemed to wither it even as I looked. The ghost was living in me now, that's what it felt like. His icy breath was mine, like the wind's icy breath was mine. The blast that withered the tree came from inside me as well as from outside the doorway.

Then, the little yellow gleam of my flashlight leading the way, I set out through the falling snow. It covered my tracks behind me. I thought it did. I hoped that it did, forever.

In that relentless veil of snow I don't know how I found my way. Perhaps the ghost found it for me. How else did I arrive in the right place, hardly knowing I was going there? It took an hour, at least, in that dreadful weather.

I climbed over the fence. I pulled at the stones Zakky and I had worked so hard to loosen, and sure enough they came away at once as we had expected they would do. There was a rusty grating underneath. When I pulled it, it came away quite easily, to my surprise. A deep black hole gaped in the white snow. Shining my flashlight down, I saw the shaft reaching away, with rusty iron rungs set into it for handholds and footholds. I took a breath; now it was my turn to journey to the center of the earth, and God knows what I would find there — worse things than dinosaurs, probably.

"Coming," I said aloud, turning my face upward. The snow had almost stopped falling. The odd star glittering above me, I could feel the air growing icier by the minute as a few stray snowflakes settled gently one by one on my blubber earthling lips, on my bony nose and jelly eyes, on my mysterious lashes and even more mysterious earthling eyebrows.

"I'm coming," I said, then let myself down into the darkness.

# 13

## BECKY

When I came down that morning — that awful morning — the front door was open again. I'd known it would be. At the same time I knew that wasn't the reason I'd woken, shivering. I almost dreaded coming downstairs, in fact, despite the gray and white snow world outside my window; normally the first snow of winter would have had me rushing excitedly for my toboggan. It was true that though we have snow in Derbyshire most years, we don't normally have such snow, such bitter cold, till well into the new year, or at least till after Christmas.

My father was in the hall staring fixedly at something. I wondered why he hadn't shut the door until I saw what he was staring at: the Christmas tree, or rather what had been the Christmas tree. The lights were still strung all over it, still glittering. Colored balls still hung from some boughs, the peacock stood on top, his tail proudly spread. But they hung, stood, glittered, on bare, not to say skeletal, branches — the few pine needles remaining were brown, not green — all the rest lay in drifts across the floor. Yesterday's live tree looked as if it had been dead forever.

It was not surprising, I suppose, in the circumstances, that no one noticed Will's absence at first. At breakfast my parents reflected on the effects of icy winds on trees in warm houses. How else could they explain it? But they hardly sounded convinced. After a while their voices died away and we sat in stunned silence looking at our plates.

Then my mother looked at my father and said pleadingly, "You can't think it was Will who opened that door, can you, not any longer? How could any boy be responsible for that?"

It was the nearest she'd gotten, the nearest she ever got to admitting, out loud, that the strange things that had happened in our house those months couldn't just have been normal human kinds of things. Perhaps it's harder for grown-ups to believe in ghosts. Perhaps it's more frightening for them in some ways. Or perhaps they just don't know how to believe in them. They didn't know how to deal with them, for sure, any more than I did.

My father, of course, was having none of it. He said, "Where *is* the wretched boy?"

"Still asleep, I suppose," my mother said, sighing. "Perhaps you'd better go and wake him, Becky." But then she added, "No, don't. Leave him. He got himself in such a state last night, I'm sure he needs his sleep.

When I looked in on him just now he was dead to the world. Probably overexcitement did it. He was very good, wasn't he, as Buttons? I must say I was proud of him, as proud as I was of you, duck."

A few weeks ago I might have found this an objectionable statement. Not any longer. With a feeling of sudden premonition I could not begin to explain, I said, "He looked so sad as Buttons, he used to make me cry sometimes. Are you sure he's all right? Hadn't I better go and see?" I got to my feet, but my mother beckoned me back.

"Don't, Becky. He just made a mess of his room and went to sleep, that's all," she insisted. "He's been so tired lately. Leave him to sleep."

And so I did. Afterward I wished I hadn't. It was almost midday before my mother went into his room and discovered there were only pillows under his duvet. At once she started organizing the search in what had always used to be her normal efficient way. But there was no sign of him anywhere in the house or garden either, though we looked everywhere.

"Try Zakky," I said desperately, when she asked me, at last, her voice tight, where else I thought he could have gone. "Zakky's the only person he talks to these days." (Well, not talk exactly, I thought, but did not know how to say.)

But though Zakky was at home when my mother rang, he could not help. He said he hadn't heard a word from Will. So my mother rang my father, who said ring the police. The police said ring Ms. Simms, maybe he's gone to London. Mum rang Ms. Simms. But Ms. Simms hadn't heard anything either. Not yet, anyway.

"The police think I may be worrying too soon," Mum said. "Boys do run away sometimes after family arguments. All he had to do was walk down the hill and get the little train to Derby, and from there the train to London."

"In *this* weather?" I asked, frantic with worry. Thinking of SOS messages. So-and-so last heard of . . . Megan, for instance.

"He took proper clothes, Becky. I've checked that — Oh, if only . . ." My mother stopped and gave such a sigh. I wonder now if she, too, had been thinking of Megan. "Oh, if only . . ." Why was she so calm? I wondered. I wished she wouldn't be. In a way it made me worry more than ever.

Zakky turned up a little while later, though we hadn't been expecting him and had certainly not expected him so soon. Anyone would have thought he really was the Angel Gabriel, complete with wings. In fact he'd been lucky, had just caught a train about to leave Matlock, then hitched a lift up the hill. What he told us about Will and the shaft made my mother ring the police again. Then she and I and Zakky set out through the snow toward Knob Farm. The road was all right, surprisingly, though the salted slush left tide marks on our boots. Derbyshire is always good about clearing roads in winter — it helps that the chief constable used to live in our village. The track up to Knob Farm had been partly cleared with a tractor, also. It did not take us much longer than usual to get that far.

Beyond Knob Farm was a different matter. The snow lay thick and untouched with a coating of ice on top that crunched as we broke through it. Clearly no one had walked there since the snow stopped falling. Even so I could have sworn I saw blurred tracks in places that might have been made by someone going this way during the snowfall. The snow had mostly blotted them out, but not entirely.

They were quite small tracks, so far as it was possible to tell; small enough to have been made by Will. I don't know whether that possibility more reassured or frightened me. Frightened me probably, thinking of that mine shaft ahead of us, of Will and who knows who else being down it.

We must have been quite a sight, the three of us: my mother and me, fat with woolen and padded jackets and trousers and big woolly hats pulled down over freezing ears, tall Zakky, whom no amount of padding could make look anything but skinny, making our way in line, footstep by laborious footstep, toward the fenced mound that contained the shaft.

It was not only a frosty but a foggy morning. You

couldn't see more than fifty yards or so in any direction. The sounds of our feet and voices came back at us loudly, yet also somehow as muffled as the lines of walls and trees were muffled, even quite close at hand. The hedges and trees were laden with snow, the twigs and branches that snow hadn't reached were threaded with gray-and-white cobwebs of frost. Everything was gray and white, except for us in our bright winter hats and jackets, except for the red berries on a thorn bush next to the mound. Some berries lay scattered on the ground beneath, split, the seeds spilling out, red juice staining the white snow, while all about the snow was scored with the scratchy little tracks of the birds that had been gorging on them till we came. We had seen them fly up as we struggled toward them. We heard their thin, high voices calling from the bushes round us.

Not that we took any notice. Even before we had climbed the fence to the mound we could see where Will had pulled the stones back; we could see the gaping hole in the ground.

The police arrived not long after, two carloads of them, both with blue lights spinning and sirens blaring. Then came the pothole rescue people in their strong plastic coats and trousers, big boots and woolly hats, carrying ropes and chains and lamps, hooks and grapples, picks and spades. Two men, one in a green striped hat, another in a plain khaki one, climbed down into the shaft. They didn't come up for what seemed ages.

They hadn't gotten Will, of course. In my heart of hearts I'd known they wouldn't have. There'd been a rockfall in the tunnel the shaft reached to, they couldn't get beyond it, they told us; no one could get beyond it without specialized digging gear.

Let's hope Will wasn't under the rockfall, they said. If he had been, he hadn't a hope in hell. If he was beyond it, assuming there was air in the tunnel he'd be all right for a while. Goodness knows, though, how long it would take to reach him. Sometimes it took three hours, sometimes three days or longer. It all depended. Let's hope he was a tough lad as well as a stupid one. Assuming he was still alive, they added dourly; they'd called and called him. But he hadn't answered, not so they could hear him anyway, though they had listened carefully.

He'd picked his time, then, hadn't he? They said ruefully, looking up at the sky. Let's hope it doesn't start snowing again. Then we'll be in real trouble.

Zakky turned his back on us and wandered away a little. I wondered if he was praying. I know I felt like praying. I looked at my mother meanwhile. Her face red with cold and maybe more, she looked back at me steadily for a minute. Then she put her arms round me, at the same time I put my arms round her. We didn't say anything. But though, with all her thick clothes on especially, my arms wouldn't nearly go round her, though her big arms enclosed me entirely, it felt as if she needed my comfort as much I needed hers. I was much too busy weeping for Will to have time to think whether I liked that — maybe I didn't entirely.

Well, you know how these things are. I dare say you've heard many such stories on radio and television, in the daily papers. "Boy missing." "Boy lost in cave/up cliff/down shaft." "Family weeps." "Community waits with bated breath," and so on.

Mum and Megan had only been worth a radio SOS message. Will, on the other hand, made the lot, first the local radio and television news, next day the national radio and television news. He was in all the papers. One day he was headlines in the *Daily Mail*. That was my fault entirely.

"LOST BOY ON GHOST HUNT" it thundered. The fact was I'd been so worried and unhappy and the reporter had been so nice to me, sharing his sandwiches, offering me his handkerchief when I started to cry, giving me a can of Coke, that I'd ended up telling him the whole story. There was a picture alongside the story to make things worse. The caption underneath read "Pretty Rebecca Fox (14) weeps for her cousin," and there was I, sure enough, sniveling into the dire reporter's handkerchief, though so far as I knew at the time there hadn't been a photographer in sight. In the circumstances I wasn't even pleased at being described as pretty, and fourteen instead of thirteen.

Again, you know how it is with these things. Though afterward it seemed to have lasted no time at all, while you're living it the nightmare goes on forever. Every minute crawls by. A whole hour seems like a week.

Of course, we didn't spend all our time up by the shaft, though I would have, I think, if my mother had let me. But she wouldn't, she said there was no point, especially after what I'd said to the man from the *Daily Mail*. So I sat and watched television or tried to, trying to forget the scene up there; the cars and vans parked in the farmyard, the snow gray and trampled, quite worn away in most places, gray spikes of winter grass sticking up miserably wherever you looked. There were still red berries on the thorn bushes — what with the crowds of people at all times, the birds had given up entirely; the men had rigged up floodlights, and even at night the work went on.

Apart from the television crews, the radio reporters, the newspapermen, the police, the rescue teams, there were also the sightseers — oh, yes, the sightseers came in droves. When the police stopped them walking up past Knob Farm, they came the other way, through the fields in the valley, past the little wood, up the slope that had been covered in bracken in August; nothing could stop them, certainly not the snow and cold, though the police had erected barriers to keep them from getting in the way of the rescue workers.

All the time, of course, I thought about Will. If he was alive down there still, and if so, if they could get him out before he starved to death. Or else died from lack of air. Part of me feared he must be dead already, but I didn't like to think of that. I wouldn't think of it, I kept on hoping, imagining over and over the moment they brought him up again; though looking like one dead already, he'd open his eyes and say, "Hello, Becky." Or better still, "Hello, Becks."

Sometimes I was angry more than anything else: with Will for being so stupid as to go down there, or at any rate to go down without having told me he was going to; with myself for having been so wrapped up in being Cinderella, for being so happy and excited during the performance I'd forgotten all about him except as Buttons; with the reporters for making such a nuisance of themselves; with the rescuers for being so slow — it would have taken Will a few minutes to get down there, how could it be taking three days so far to get him out? (Even though I knew they had to work slowly because of the danger of more rockfalls, and so on.)

I was even angry with Zakky Thompson. He came up every day to see us. Aunt Maggie said, "Let him come. He's Will's friend." But it was easy for her to say, it wasn't her he clung to. The first time he brought two buttons for me, Jesus Lives and Jesus Saves.

"Let's hope he does save," I said crossly, taking them reluctantly, wanting to cry for some reason, at the same time terrified Zakky would offer to say a prayer with me; he had been known to offer such comforts in the past. Well, some people said so. If so I had to believe them; the third time Zakky came he did actually offer to kneel down and pray with me for Will.

I turned red and shrugged my shoulders. "I'd rather not."

"Okay then," said Zakky in his deep voice, but he spent the rest of the morning picking out hymn tunes on the old piano in the dining room which hadn't been touched since I gave up lessons yonks ago. He might be able to sing, but he'd no more talent for the piano than I had, judging by the sounds he made. He must have known the notes, though, to be able to pick out the tunes from the tatty old hymnbook that had lain on top of the piano all my life, along with the books containing the pieces I'd struggled through; I don't know where it came from.

When he arrived at "Rock of Ages Cleft for Me, Let Me Hide Myself in Thee," I'd had enough and said so. Zakky looked at me with his bright blue eyes and agreed that these words were a bit much in the circumstances. It was at this moment I realized he was almost as worried as I was. I don't know why I hadn't realized it before, unless it was because Zakky's face never seemed to change much, whatever he was thinking. I almost said he could pray with me now if he wanted, but then I thought better of it. It wasn't that I didn't want to pray or hadn't been praying all the time. "Oh, God," I was praying, "please make Will come out alive. Oh, God, I'll believe in you forever if you do. Oh, God, I love Will, he's my brother, keep him safe." It was just that on the whole I preferred to pray in silence by myself, not embarrassingly, out loud, with Zakky.

I had completely forgotten about it being Christmas. Everyone had. The withered tree had been cleared from the hall the first day, and no one had had the heart to replace it.

On the fourth morning I got up very early, before my parents, to find my mother's newspaper lying on the hall floor, under the letterbox. The headline read: "Hope fading for Pit Boy. Rescuers meet another setback."

That was enough for me. I didn't even bother to turn on the radio or television news to see if anything had changed since the article was written. Shrugging on my boots and hat and jacket, I crept out of the house and set off up the hill.

It was yet another bright, crisp morning, the way it had been every morning since that first gray, foggy one. The snow was a cruel blue and frost glittered relentlessly from all the trees and hedges.

At the bottom of the track to Knob Farm I met Zakky Thompson, who smiled his lopsided smile at me but didn't say anything, though he must have noticed Jesus Lives pinned defiantly to my jacket. What I meant, of course, was Will Lives. But I didn't tell him; I don't suppose he would have approved. I don't suppose any religious people would, I thought, as we trudged up the icy track together in silence. The police had salted the track by then. Police cars had skidded a few times, it was said, before they'd gotten round to it. Coming down — it was a steep track — a few people on foot had fallen over.

We had barely reached the top of the track when we heard a police siren. We thought it was a police siren. But when we turned back to look, we saw an ambulance tearing up the track toward us, throwing up the salted slush.

Zakky and I looked at each other. We waited for the ambulance to pass, then with one accord started hurrying as fast as we were able. The police knew who we were, they didn't stop us. We arrived at the shaft, ducking between the press people and the telly people, just in time to see the stretcher being carried toward the ambulance waiting at the final gate before the track ended, its doors open.

"Let me see, he's my cousin, let me see!" Though one policeman did try to stop me this time, he didn't try hard enough. I reached the ambulance doors at the same time as the stretcher just in time to see Will's face, precisely as I had imagined seeing it all those days. His face, though, wasn't a bit as I had imagined. It was as gray as the gray snow on the trampled grass. Nor did he smile at me; how could he, his eyes were closed, he couldn't see me. I might even have thought him dead, except for the fact they hadn't covered up his face with a blanket the way they'd covered up his pathetically thin little body. I'd seen enough disasters on television to know that when people were dead they blanketed them up entirely and didn't leave any faces showing.

I burst into tears at that moment, just as my mother and father arrived, clinging to each other, a fact I saw with approval, blood being thicker than water. The police had called them, I suppose; the rescuers must have been able to signal they were bringing Will up shortly. Only my father stayed with me, however. My mother went with Will in the ambulance — in some ways, of course, I minded this a lot. At the same time I didn't mind at all, because of my relief that they had found him, also because of the way that my father almost forgot his dislike of messy situations for once and tucked his arm quite tightly around my shoulder.

I could still hardly believe what had happened. Though the tears were pouring down my cheeks, I felt as flat and white as a newly washed bath towel. The anger I'd felt seeing the ambulance doors close on my mother and my cousin was more relief than anything. Gray as he'd looked, unconscious as he'd looked, I already knew for sure Will was going to be all right.

And I tell you how I knew. It was because something — someone — else had been brought up the shaft with him, wrapped in a gray blanket. And because, in my hearing, the big potholer in the green-striped hat had described to anyone who wanted to listen exactly how they had found Will; how he lay just as he would have wanted, curled up in a small rock cavity, holding in his arms, as if it were the other half of his own body, the skeleton of a boy only a little smaller than he was.

"MIRACLE BOY SURVIVES. BONES MYSTERY. GHOST MYSTERY — DID BONES BOY SPEAK THE TRUTH?" were the headlines next morning. But I wasn't interested in them, not any longer.

He was tough all right, my cousin Will. Or maybe the real healing had been done earlier, in the rockshaft, so that what the hospital had to cure him of — exhaustion, cold, hunger — was a cinch by comparison, dead easy at any rate. They let him out after only two days; though he was thinner than ever, in some ways he looked better than I'd seen him. Maybe it was because he almost looked peaceful. Or maybe I was just used to the way he looked in general.

Only one thing still worried him. He'd gone on and on about it, my mother said, from the moment he first woke up in the hospital. In fact, since the skeleton was at once proved to be an old one and the police weren't looking for a murderer or anything, it wasn't difficult to arrange matters as he wanted. We were able to bury Will's ghost before Christmas even, on Christmas Eve, in the old burial ground just up the hill from our house, almost in sight of Will's bedroom window, to the sound not of hymns, let alone carols, but of the rooks cawing and flapping before they went to rest.

"Dust to dust," said the clergyman on that cold afternoon, under a yellow sky threatening still more snow to follow, and in the presence of me, Will, Zakky, my father and mother, and a phalanx of reporters and photographers and television cameras. "Dust to dust. Ashes to ashes." I admit I wept a little as the small coffin was lowered into the grave. I wept for a boy who had lived more than a hundred years ago, whom I hadn't known or seen ever, except perhaps, had I but known it at the time, as a ghost face in a window. I wept a little for Will too — not that I need have done, judging by his face. Though there were tears pouring down it I knew his ghost was laid — well, one of his ghosts at least. (Some other kinds of hauntings, I was beginning to realize, looking at my mother, are more likely to last a lifetime.)

"BURY ME" the coins from my purse had demanded. And so, at last, we had done so, just as the snow began to fall. Of course the grave hadn't a headstone yet, but my mother was going to order one after Christmas. There was to be no name on it, no date either; on

Will's urgent insistence there would be written only "R.I.P."

I don't know how my mother managed it, but she had achieved miracles in every way you could imagine. When Mr. Hapgood the clergyman, Zakky, Will, me, her, and my father arrived back at our house for tea after the funeral, leaving the press behind us, we found a new green Christmas tree filling the hall with its glitter and marvel.

We were snowed up on Christmas Day. Despite the remaining sadness — at different times I happened on both Will and my mother looking with melancholy faces through the blue and red photograph albums and couldn't prevent a small pang of jealousy — it was the best Christmas ever. I know Will thought so. He and I even managed to quarrel a little, over who got the gun and who the rope in the game of Clue that Dad had given him. I mean things were really getting back to normal.

Will's present to me, by the way, was a Dire Straits record that, from his hospital bed, he'd begged my mother to get me. I gave him a Ray Bradbury anthology I knew he wanted. Inside I wrote, "For my saved-from-the-dead cousin Will, with lots and lots of love from Becks." I'd added about ten XXXs, and as I was writing them I remember thinking that my mother was right. That, without any doubt whatever, blood really must be thicker than water.

(Apart from anything else, between Will's coming and Christmas I lost fifteen pounds without even trying, and it was mostly due to him. I was *thin* almost. Oh, glory!)